SEVENTH GENERATION

STEVE PRENTICE

Relax. Read. Repeat.

SEVENTH GENERATION
By Steve Prentice
Published by TouchPoint Press
Brookland, AR 72417
www.touchpointpress.com

Copyright © 2021 Steve Prentice
All rights reserved.

ISBN 978-1-952816-59-8

Editor: Jenn Haskin
Cover Design: Colbie Myles
Cover Illustration: Taylor Gillion

Connect with the author:
https://www.goodreads.com/StevePrentice

steve.prentice.75   StevePrentice7   @prentice.striks

First Edition

Library of Congress Control Number: 2021940618

Young Adult Fiction / Magical Realism /Mythology / Native American

Printed in the United States of America.

To my wife and daughter for their endless assistance
and patience with this project.

CHAPTER ONE

MARCUS AND I HAVE BEEN OFF and on friends since we started eighth grade this year. The glance Marcus gave me left little doubt what was coming as he walked by. The sharp blow to the back of my head from his knuckles stung all the way through to my eyeballs. I thought they were going to shoot out my nose. My head was swirling in pain as I lunged out of my chair, digging my thumbs deep into Marcus's throat. Marcus came around with a forearm smash to my head sending me into the file cabinet. I charged back at Marcus and we both tumbled under the teacher's desk. By the time the crisis workers pulled me off Marcus, he had blood dripping down the side of his cheek where one of my fingernails had caught his skin and a small knot was beginning to form on his forehead where I had thrown him to the floor.

My chest heaved as I tried to catch my breath under the heavy weight of Mr. Johns' arms. "Just relax," he whispered. I felt like my chest was caving in. My head spun. *I could feel the flames starting to shoot out my nose, scorching the floor. Oh, no. Not yet. I can't change now. I could feel the rough scales forming and the blaze burning deep in my chest, forcing its way to the surface.*

"Hold on, Trae," Mr. Johns said. "We will get you up to the office soon, just let us clear the hall." *How could Mr. Johns not feel my skin starting to change? He was surely going to notice as I stretched out and began to grow to the size of a giant tree trunk. I looked down and could see my arms retreat into my serpent body as the rings began to form. I could feel the horns pushing their way*

1

through the scales on my head and my body begin to swell and stretch. Mr. Johns struggled to keep hold as my body swelled; his arms straining to keep from slipping off the side. The flames in my chest glowed bright as I raised my head and looked down at the frightened crisis workers. My horns scraped across the ceiling, knocking out tiles as I turned and slithered towards the door. I could feel Mr. Johns slowly slide off my side as I entered the hallway.

The hallway was buzzing with energy as Mr. Johns barked directions at the other staff to keep students from being crushed or eaten. "Get those kids away from the door and down the hall. Open the front door, let's drive it outside!" I slithered towards the door as sparks shot from my scales, causing the children to whimper as my massive body towered over them.

"Keep Marcus back in the classroom until we get this thing out of here," Mr. Johns said, as he slammed the classroom door behind me. The janitor tried to prod me towards the door, but the handle of his mop snapped off between the sharp scales of my body. I slithered to the front door before rising and turning my head back toward the hall. A small jet of flame gave notice that I was not to be followed. I turned out onto 16th street and headed towards the subterranean world of the subways. [1]

THE WELTS FROM MARCUS' fingernails burning across my chest brought me back to reality as I sat slumped over in the corner of the empty time out room. Mr. Johns was resting against the opposite wall, staring out the fenced window above my head. I raised my eyes slowly trying not to catch his gaze. He caught my look and gave me a warm smile, "Welcome back, Trae. You have been gone for a while. Did you have a nice trip?"

I tried to fake a smile. I knew he was trying to lighten the mood, but it always made me angry when he poked fun at my daydreams.

Mr. Corfa knocked on the door and stuck his head
wanted on the phone, Mr. Johns. It is Marcus' father,"
stepped in to take Mr. Johns' place keeping watch over me. Mr.
Corfa was a very tall, thin man with a thick African accent. I charged
the door as Mr. Johns walked out, but Mr. Corfa stepped in front of
it and held me off until the door was closed. I pushed against Mr.
Corfa as I pulled at the doorknob trying to get out of the room, but
seeing as he was three people bigger than me, it didn't really work.
I decided to move on to my cage match.

*The first thing you want to do in a cage match is jump up on the
fence on the window, which really gets the crowd going. Pulling on it
makes a good racket, but the crowd gets super pumped if you bang
on it. You always want to keep one eye out for "the Mangler," you
don't want him sneaking up and smashing you with a folding chair.
Now once you get the crowd good and wild, you can always tell
because Mr. Corfa buries his head in his hands, you have to crouch
down sumo-style and start taunting the Mangler. The thing about the
Mangler is that he is fast, you have to have eyes on him, or he will
come flying at you off a top rope. I usually like to start with a good
flying elbow to the chin then maybe a good scissor kick to the back of
the head.*

*Once you get the Mangler on the ground he is easy prey. I
always circle slowly, to get the crowd wound up before giving him
the old splash move across the chest. Of course, every once in a
while, you go for that move and the mangy beast moves before you
get there. Such was the case on this day. I climbed up to the top
rope, raised my hands to the roaring crowd, then jumped through
the air only to land hard on the mat. As I rolled over all blurry-
eyed, I saw the Mangler coming off the top rope with an elbow
smash. It's too late, I was out.*

I don't know how long I was out, but when I came to, Mr. Johns
was standing over me with that same warm, half smile that never
seems to leave his face, no matter how many times I have screwed up.

"You ready to give the counselors' room a shot, Trae?" Mr. Johns asked. "I think it's time to give the Mangler a break for a while."

Mr. Johns reached out and pulled me to my feet. I felt a little lightheaded and a lot charged up. I, of course, could not let the Mangler know he had gotten the best of me, so I strutted out of the ring, trying not to limp.

We walked across the hall to the counselors' room. Marcus was still sitting in one corner, slouched over in boredom until he caught sight of me coming in. As I walked by, he swung at me with his foot, almost making contact before Mr. Corfa could push his chair back.

"Come on man, you were doing fine a minute ago. Do not lose it now!" Mr. Corfa said. "I was about to let you go to lunch, but you are not ready yet, are you? I guess you will be having lunch with us today."

Marcus gave me a little smile out of the side of his mouth, knowing he had just missed. Mr. Johns led me to the other side of the room, away from Marcus, like I couldn't be across the room as soon as he turned his back. Silly man! I sat in the chair giving Marcus the stink eye before smiling back at him. Marcus and I are actually friends most of the time but sometimes we like to scrap with each other, especially when he is being a pain.

"You know I have to call your father now Trae," Mr. Johns said. "When you draw blood, we have to call your parents." Mr. Johns picked up the phone and dialed my father's cell phone. I could hear my father's annoyance as soon as he picked up.

"What now?"

"Hello, Mr. Chadwick, this is Mr. Johns from your son's school."

"I know bloody well who it is. What did Trae do now?"

I never understood why my father thought he needed to talk like a Brit, everyone knew he was Cherokee.

"Well, Mr. Chadwick, your son got into a fight today with one of his friends and he scratched the kid across the cheek, drawing blood."

"What is my kid doing in your school if you people cannot keep him under control? I don't have time for this nonsense. I have investors breathing down my neck, I don't need this aggravation."

"I understand, Mr. Chadwick, but our school policy requires us to inform the parents when there is a fight that results in an injury."

"Well, is the other boy all right?"

"Yes sir, we patched him up. He will be fine."

"Can you put Trae on the phone for me?"

Mr. Johns held out the phone to me. I tried to feign fear, but I don't think Mr. Johns was buying it. "Hi, dad."

"What is wrong with you, boy?"

"I don't know. I'm broken, I guess."

"You guess? No TV and no video games when you get home, Trae. You have lost your privileges!"

I don't even remember the last time I had "privileges," I thought to myself. "All right, sure, dad."

"Don't 'sure' me. We are going to talk about this when I get home."

"All right."

Click.

"I think he wants to talk to you, Mr. Johns," I said, as I handed the phone back to him. Mr. Johns was not amused.

I spent the rest of the day in time out, making eyes at everyone who walked by the office while Mr. Johns helped me with my schoolwork. At the end of the day Mr. Johns walked me to the door. "Tomorrow is a fresh start, Trae. Let's make it a good day," Mr. Johns said with his familiar warm smile. "Have a good night, son."

CHAPTER TWO

WHEN I GOT HOME DAD WAS, of course, still working until who knows when. So I grabbed myself a pop tart and flipped on the TV. There is never anything on during the day except a bunch of whiny people fighting in front of a fake judge about who stole whose boyfriend first as they try to explain why they threw a rock through someone's windshield. Sometimes those catfights can be a lot of fun, but today it just wasn't getting it done.

I found myself staring out the window down at Central Park and the craggy black stone outcrops that had become my playground. I imagined they were the Black Hills of South Dakota where Sitting Bull took a stand. One of the only interesting things my teacher had ever told us about.

I decided to go down and do a little search and destroy mission at the rock. I left the TV on so the stupid girls could fight it out while I was gone. I hopped the elevator down to the lobby where Eddy, the doorman, is always sorting the mail.

"Hey, little man Trae! How's it today?" he asked, with the type of enthusiasm only a doorman can fake.

I gave him our ritual fist bump as I ran out the door and onto Central Park West. The thick smell of the subway and traffic hit me as I sucked as much air into my lungs as I could. I let out a giant belch before bursting across the street, completely unaware of the stalled traffic. I jumped over the small cobblestone wall and into the park.

I walked through the trees and bushes towards the black

outcrops, carefully avoiding contact with the spies that would surely give me away to the enemy. I must take the high ground before they realize I am coming. I edged my way out carefully along the steep backside of the largest outcrop, where I could get a good view of all the enemy positions. I liked to lay looking over the top of the ridge, searching the horizon for the enemy's heavy armor. I listened carefully for any sounds of the enemy trying to sneak up for a side attack.

As the sun began to set, the faint sound of drums softly echoed off the black stone. There are many strange sounds in Central Park at dusk to be sure, but something about these drums demanded my attention.

Unable to contain my curiosity, I peered carefully off the edge to where the sound seemed to be coming from. The sound seemed to be getting louder and louder as it started echoing in my head. I leaned out as far as I could, but I still could not see where the sound was coming from. I stretched out with every fiber I had making myself as long as I could, but I was still not able to see the source of the sound now pounding in my head. I tumbled over the edge, crashing through branches that tore at my clothing and ripped my skin. My first solo flight ended with a loud thump and a low moan. The final insult came when the Jolly Ranchers I had stolen from Mr. Johns' office earlier fell out of my pocket and onto the ground. Definitely not my best landing.

My head was spinning but at least it silenced the echoing of the drums. I was perfectly content to just lay there, moaning to myself, until I got the strange feeling that I was not alone in the thick underbrush. The dull pain rolled around as I slowly turned my head. Two beautiful black eyes framed by dark mossy skin, which almost blended perfectly with the stone, opened wide and then blinked in shock. I turned away not wanting to believe what my blurry eyes had just seen.

I lay there for a while not sure if I dared to look again, partially afraid they would still be there and partially afraid they wouldn't. I finally mustered the strength to turn my head back towards where I had seen the eyes. Not only were the eyes gone, so were my Jolly Ranchers!

What an insult!

I figured I might as well just lie there for a while longer, or at least until the trees stopped spinning anyway. I decided I probably should think about getting up when I realized it was getting too dark to even see the tops of the trees. I got to my feet, my head still spinning, and decided it might be better to walk around the wall then try to scale over it this time.

When I entered the lobby, Eddy looked a little shocked and concerned with my appearance. I, of course, had to put a brave face on it. "They tried to get the best of me, Eddy, but the Forlorn will never take me alive!" In case you don't know, and I am not sure how you couldn't, the Forlorn are the enemy in Horror, which is just the best video game ever. Eddy gave me a doubtful look, "Good night, Mr. Trae."

I stumbled up to our apartment, hoping that my father was not home yet, or hoping if he was, he was already too drunk to notice me come in. My father always talked about his brother being nothing but a stinking drunk who never got off the reservation, but from where I stood my father and his snobby friends smelled about the same as I remember my uncle smelling when I was little. According to my cousin, my uncle had cleaned himself up and had started dancing, which is more then I could say about my father and his supposedly "high-class" friends sipping their cheap wine, looking down their noses at the people passing by below.

I had gotten myself so riled up thinking about it, that I flung the door open and marched my little old bad self inside only to find that my father was not even home yet. Feeling a little silly I went into the bathroom, stripped down, stuffed my clothes deep into the laundry basket where my father would not see them, and went to bed as the steam from my little rampage faded away.

CHAPTER THREE

AS I SETTLED INTO BED, my little tumble at the park crept back into my mind. I tried to shake off the eyes in the bushes, but to say I had some strange dreams would be a bit of an understatement. I dreamt about a sorcerer named Glooscap, from some of the old stories my mom used to tell me.

When we last left our hero, as they like to say in tales such as this, Glooscap was standing in a village listening to a story from a man who seemed very scared. A monster had stopped the flow and spoiled the waters of the nearby stream. The man told of going up stream to find out why the beautiful fresh spring water had stopped flowing to their village. He set out in hopes of stopping the suffering of his people. He told of how he walked a long time until he finally came to a village. The people of the village were not like the people of his village; they had webbed hands and feet. The stream widened out and had a little bit of water still left in it. It was yellowish and slimy but the man was thirsty, so he asked for a drink, even if the water was bad.

"We cannot give you water," the people with the webbed hands and feet said. "Our big chief wants it all for himself, so unless he permits it there will be no water for you."

"Where is your chief?" the man said as bravely as he could.

"You must follow the stream further into the woods, but we must warn you not to drink without first asking the big chief."

The man told of how he walked on, deep into the woods,

9

following the spoiled water until he finally came upon the big chief. The once brave man trembled with fear because the big chief was an enormous monster, so big that if you stood at his feet you would not be able to see his head. He filled the whole valley from one end to the other. The monster had dug himself a giant hole and dammed it up so all the water would flow into the hole and none of it could escape into the stream. He had fouled the water so that a stinky slime covered its entire surface.

This enormous monster had a grin that went from ear to ear. His bulging yellow eyes stared out of his head like huge pine knots. The monster studied the man for what seemed like a thousand years until he finally said in a loud croak, "Little man, what do you want?"

The trembling man said, "I come from a village where our only stream has run dry because you are keeping all the water for yourself. We would like it if you would allow us to have some of the water and to please not muddy it so much that no one can drink it."

The Monster blinked at him a few times before croaking:

Do as you please
Do as you please

I don't care
I don't care

If you want water
If you want water

Go elsewhere.

The man said, "We need water. Our people are dying."

The Monster croaked:

I don't care
I don't care
Go away stop bothering me
Go away stop bothering me

Go away
Go away

Or I will eat you whole.

The monster opened his mouth wide and inside it the man could see the many things the monster had killed. The monster gulped a few times and smacked his lips with a noise that sounded like thunder.

At this point the man's courage finally broke and he turned and ran as fast as he could. He could hear the croaking laughter of the monster ringing in his ears as he ran back to his village.

This is a long dream, but this is where it really gets crazy. *Crazier you say?* I know, but just wait.

As Glooscap listened to this tale, he became more and more concerned and more and more enraged. So Glooscap prepared himself for war. He painted himself red, the color of blood. He made himself twelve feet tall. He used two huge clamshells for his earrings. He put a hundred black eagle feathers and a hundred white eagle feathers in his scalp lock. He painted yellow circles around his eyes. He twisted his mouth into a fearsome snarl. He stomped his feet and the earth trembled. He uttered his war cries and they echoed off the mountains over and over again. He took a huge mountain of flint and made a knife as sharp as a weasel's tooth.

"Now I am going," he said as he walked off in giant strides that sounded like thunder and lightening, mighty eagles circling over his head. This is how Glooscap came to the village of the people with webbed feet and hands.

"I want water," he said as the people looked upon him with great fear. They brought him a little muddy water. "I think I will get more water and cleaner water," he said as he stomped off up stream.

He confronted the monster. "I want clean water," he said. "Lots of it for the people downstream."

Ho! Ho!
Ho! Ho!

All the water is mine
All the water is mine

Go away
Go away

Or I will kill you

"Slimy clump of mud!" Glooscap cried. "We will see who gets killed!"

As they fought the mountains rumbled and the ground broke open. Mighty trees were splintered into toothpicks. The monster opened his mouth wide to swallow Glooscap, but Glooscap made himself taller than the tallest trees and even the monster's mile wide mouth was not big enough to swallow him. Glooscap gripped his mighty knife made of flint and slit the monsters bloated belly open wide. From the wound flowed a mighty stream, then a roaring river that tumbled and foamed as it gouged out a large riverbed for itself, down past the village and on to the great sea.

"There, that should be enough water for the people!" Glooscap said.

He grabbed the monster and squeezed it ever smaller until he *had squeezed the giant creature into a small bullfrog before flinging it into the swamp.*[2]

As I would find out later, the reason that a bullfrog's skin is supposedly so wrinkled is because Glooscap squeezed so hard.

CHAPTER FOUR

BY THE TIME I WOKE UP in the morning, my father was already off to his "real life" on Wall Street. The only evidence that he had even been home were the burnt cigars and empty wine glasses he and his friends had left behind.

I went through my normal morning routine: getup, turn on the water in the bathroom sink, make faces at my self in the mirror, turn on the TV, and microwave a pop tart. *Why microwave a pop tart, you ask? I don't know, it doesn't matter, I won't eat it anyway.* Then I get dressed, spend twenty minutes looking for my shoes only to remember, as I slip on my dress shoes, that I had kicked them off behind the couch the night before and, oh yeah, turn off the water in the bathroom sink.

I like to take different routes to the subway everyday just to keep the Forlorn off my trail, but today I must have been distracted because by the time I realized where I was, I was already four blocks past my usual subway stop. The silly dream had mostly faded, but I could not get what happened to me at the park out of my mind. I kept thinking about that face and those big dark eyes staring at me. I knew it could not have been real, but where did the Jolly Ranchers go? I had double and triple checked my pockets this morning and they really were gone. I knew I should let it go, but I just could not shake it.

I finally made it down into the subway and to school, I was forty-five minutes late, but I did get there. When I reached the front door it was, of course, locked, so I had to ring the bell. Mr. Johns opened the door and led me straight to the timeout room without saying much. He sat me down then went out. A few minutes later he returned with a small package of sliced apples, a muffin, and a carton of milk that he handed me. "All right, eat up, Mr. Trae. You have already missed too much class today," he said.

I ate slowly because I really did not want to go to class and I liked hanging with Mr. Johns. The problem was I could only make a muffin last so long before Mr. Johns would send me off to class anyway. As I was leaving, Mr. Johns asked me, "You all right, Mr. Trae? You seem a little quiet today."

"I'm good," I said as I gave him the usual fist bump.

I must have still been a little out of it though, because I went straight to class and sat down and the next time I looked up it was already lunchtime. After lunch, we had an afternoon assembly about something or other. At the end of the day, Mr. Johns was standing by the front door telling all the kids goodbye like he usually does. As I walked out, he stopped me, "So, I didn't see you again. I'm thinking you must have had a fairly good day?"

"I guess so."

"You sure you're all right?"

"Yeah, just tired."

Mr. Johns gave me a concerned look before reaching into his sweater pocket and pulling out a few Jolly Ranchers to give me. "We will see you back here Monday morning, Trae. 8:00 a.m. not 8:45 a.m., all right?"

I nodded my head, but my mind was already miles away, thinking about the stupid face and those dark eyes. I am not sure I had really stopped thinking about them all day.

Usually I go home and play around until I get bored before I head to the park. Today I couldn't wait any longer, I had to get back there. I was so excited—until I actually reached the big black outcropping where I had been yesterday. Suddenly I was scared.

15

What if they were not there? What if they were? Did I really want to see it again?

I snuck up on the spot, got down on all fours and crawled back into the underbrush where I had fallen yesterday, watching closely for any sign of life. There was nothing except a few broken branches. I decided to lay there quietly for a while and see if anything happened. I stayed there until I could not stand it any longer. I was not sure if it had been a few minutes or an hour, but I doubt it had been an hour. I sat up disappointed and frustrated until I remembered I had the Jolly Ranchers Mr. Johns had given me.

I spread the Jolly Ranchers out close to the bush where I had seen the eyes yesterday. I lay back down roughly the way I had been yesterday or at least as best as I could remember, seeing as last time my head had been spinning a bit. I waited and waited but still nothing. Now I was frustrated and a little bored, so I decided to climb to the top of the outcrop and try to sneak up to the edge and watch from there. I pressed my belly hard against the cool black rock and slowly inched my way to the edge right above where I had left the candy. There was a moment of excitement when I realized I might look over the edge and the candy would be gone, taken as I had made my way into position.

I peered tensely over the edge, waiting to see if the bait had been stolen while I was not watching, but sadly it laid right where I had left it, not so much as a nudge from the wind. I decided to wait, this time admittedly a little more distracted, but I did wait. I waited until it became to dark too even see the candy any more before finally giving up and going home. I was so bummed that I didn't even notice Eddy at the door and did not even realize it until I was already in the elevator heading for the apartment.

What had I done wrong? I was at the right spot; the branches were all broken where I fell through. I had laid the candy close to the bushes, I had waited, but nothing. Maybe I was cracking up. My

16

teacher from the old private school my dad had sent me to had told him I was crazy, maybe she was finally right. Confused and more than a little disappointed, *in case you had not noticed*, I got undressed and went straight to bed.

I watched as a slender Indian girl, with soft dark eyes, danced under the faint moonlight in a pine grove by the shore. As she danced, I could hear a woman's voice calling to her, "Come into the lodge, Leelinau, for the Silver Moon is rising. Soon the little people will come out to play among the trees. They carry away dancing maidens." Leelinau returned sorrowfully to the lodge, for she longed to see the little people.

Leelinau' s parents worried about her because from a very young age she seemed to be drawn to the forest pines of the open shore where she would gather strange flowers and plants. She had become so engrossed by the fairy pines that her parents suspected that the spirits where enticing her to the pines and that she was under their spell.

The next morning a brave came to woo Leelinau. Her mother braided her hair and dressed her for marriage. Her mother led her out to the marriage feast. Braves, squaws and maidens came from miles around to feast and celebrate Leelinau' s upcoming marriage. Leelinau sighed and wept, and begged that she might be allowed to return to the pine grove one more time to dance. She promised she would return long before the faint moonlight showed its face. Her mother agreed to let her go one last time, since she knew Leelinau would soon be forced to marry and become a woman.

Darkness fell, and Leelinau did not return. The Moon rose and shed its white beams on the lake, but still she did not return. The villagers wandered through the grove, and sought up and down the shore, but Leelinau was gone.[3]

All right, I have to admit when I woke up, even I thought that was a really strange dream, but it was my dream. I got up and tried to just put it out of my mind and move on with my day but everywhere I turned, I could see her face. *Was she the face in the bushes?* The face in the bushes had skin that was darker and mossy, but those eyes—they certainly looked like hers.

CHAPTER FIVE

I WANDERED OFF TO SCHOOL in a half daze once again, but when I reached the doors of the school and tried to open them, they were locked, and all the lights had been turned off. *Did they all leave without me? Was this some kind of cruel joke?* Ah man! No, it's Saturday.

My head was swimming with all kinds of weird random thoughts between school, the park, and my bizarro dreams. I decided since I was close, I would go down to the new hotel in Chelsea that my cousin was working on and see him.

Asija worked high above Manhattan as a steel worker. He loves to walk steel and takes great pride in being a part of the long tradition of Mohawk Indians to "boom out," or leave the reservation to work in the steel industry. He always gets so excited when he gets to talk about our history and traditions. I loved it too because it was the only time I ever got to learn anything about our people, since my father refused to discuss it.

The crazy sounds of the construction site, mixed with the thick smell of grease from the machines, was enough to make me jump-out-of-my-skin excited. I snuck in through one of the poorly locked gates towards the back of the site and was trying to play it cool, but got caught up staring at the men walking steel hundreds of feet above me and ran right into a pole. The blow knocked me to my butt. As I watched the little birdies circling my head, I could hear the crackling laughter of the construction workers coming from every corner, but the loudest laugh came from a familiar voice as Asija came sliding down a ladder towards me.

"You all right little brave?" he said as he tried to show concern through his laughter.

"I'm all right, but that pole may need a doctor!" I snapped back, not wanting him to know it hurt.

He pulled me to my feet and started dusting me off until I pulled away and snapped, "I can do it."

Asija smiled, "So what you doing down here anyway, Trae?"

"I was bored."

"Bored? Where is your dad, does he know you're down here?"

"Oh yeah, of course! He told me to come down."

He gave me a doubtful smile but did not call my bluff. "All right little brave. Give me five minutes; I will take my break and you can buy me some lunch."

After he finished his work we wandered off into the neighborhood and found a street vendor selling tacos. Asija bought us each two tacos and we found a place to lean while we ate.

"Little brave I am very happy to see you, but why don't you tell me why you are really here?" Asija asked, "I can see all over your warrior face you have something on your mind."

I really don't think I went down there to talk about anything, but I guess my warrior face had failed me again. "I don't think I have anything to say Asija, I just wanted to hang for awhile."

"All right, but something's going on with you. You don't usually give up your Saturday war games in the park to hang with the steel walkers."

The truth is I would be down here everyday listening to his stories if I thought I could get away with it. "I just thought you might need someone to listen to you ramble that's all." *Liar, liar.*

"Well little brave what do you want to hear a story about today?"

"I want to hear a story about the little people."

"The little people?" Asija said a little puzzled as I rarely, actually never, had special requests. "Let me see, I am not sure I can remember how that one goes." Asija always liked to play like he didn't know what I was talking about. "You might have to get me started, Trae."

"Come on, Asija, don't make me beg to listen to you rattle."

Asija smiled, he knew I loved his stories, "The little people of the Cherokee, called 'Yundi Tsundi,' are a race of Spirits who live in rock caves on the mountain side. They are little fellows and ladies reaching almost to your knees. They are well shaped and handsome, with hair so long it almost touches the ground. They are extremely helpful, kind hearted, and great wonder workers. They love music and spend most of their time drumming, singing, and dancing. They have a very gentle nature but do not like to be disturbed.

"Sometimes their drums are heard in lonely places in the mountains, but it is not safe to follow the sound, for they do not like to be disturbed at home. They will throw a spell over the stranger so that he is bewildered and loses his way, and even if he does at last get back to the village he will forever be dazed.

"Sometimes they come near a house at night and the people inside hear them talking, but people must not go outside, and in the morning they will find the corn has been gathered or the field cleared as if a whole force of men had been at work. Anyone who goes outside to try and see them will die.

"When a hunter finds anything in the woods, such as a knife or trinket, he must say, 'Little people, I would like to take this,' because it may belong to them. If he does not ask the little people's permission to take it, they will throw stones at him as he tries to leave.

"Some little people are black, some are white, and some are golden like the Cherokee. Sometimes they speak in Cherokee, but at other times they speak their own language.

"The little people are here to teach us about living in harmony with nature and with other people, Trae."

"Shoot, I am going to be late. My boss is going to kill me!" Asija cried, "We will have to finish this story another time."

Asija disappeared around the corner before I could even get to my feet. I wandered around looking in all the store windows until I found the subway. I was anxious to get back to Central Park, although I am not sure what I thought I was going to find, maybe their village?

CHAPTER SIX

MY HEAD WAS BUZZING with the story. I was trying to keep it all straight, while trying to figure out what it all meant. I had this rock in my stomach from thinking I would never see that face and those beautiful eyes again. I mean come on, who even knows if I really had seen anything? I have been known to be a bit, ah let's say, crazy.

When I dashed out of the subway across the street from the entrance to Central Park, dark clouds had started to form, and the wind was blowing through the canyon of buildings like a raging hurricane. Now most people would have been wise enough to go inside and wait out the storm, but of course, I ran across the street, hopped the wall, and went straight to the rock outcropping. I flopped down onto my belly and started crawling into the bushes where I had seen the eyes.

I rummaged through the bushes and past the recently discarded garbage of the mindless masses, but nothing but bushes and more bushes. I dug down through the leaves but still nothing. I laid there, panting with adrenaline and exhaustion. The pain from the belly flop burned my stomach. I must be missing something; I know I am not crazy, well, I don't think I am crazy.

The wind was blowing leaves and dirt into my eyes and mouth. I could feel the rain begin to pelt me in the back of the head. I scrambled on hands and knees over to hide at the bottom of the black stone. It was not much use by this time since it was already pouring down rain; the clouds had opened up like a busted mop bucket. I tried to push myself up under a small ledge, determined to wait it out and not abandon my search.

I waited until a small stream of rainwater invaded my hiding spot and water from the ledge above started dripping down on my head. I was quickly soaked through to my boxers and freezing cold, so I decided to make a break for home. I think I must have hit every puddle in the park on the way.

Eddy stopped me at the door before I could go slip sliding down the hall and into the elevator. "All right Trae, why don't you stand on the mat here, I will pull you out a nice dry towel, and you can dry yourself off before you go getting my nice lobby all muddy and wet." I had this image in my head of Eddy shaking me off out the door and stuffing me in the umbrella rack. I have to admit the large towel felt really good as I dried off my head and wrapped it around me on my way up to the apartment.

Because of the storm outside, the apartment seemed really dark for the middle of the day. So of course, I went around and turned all the lights on, you know, just in case. I tried the TV, but the storm had knocked the cable out and I had broken the controller for the game yesterday when I stepped on it on the way in. *Oh, did I forget to mention that I am a klutz sometimes?*

I sat in my dad's armchair by the window and watched the rain pour down, keeping an eye on the park and the black outcropping that you could just see peeking through the trees. Not sure what I thought they were going to do, dance maybe, but I watched just the same. That got pretty old pretty fast, so I decided to move onto indoor adventure since the park was obviously not going to be happening.

I dug under my bed for lost soldiers of past epic wars with the Forlorn. I recovered the remains of these brave green plastic heroes and gave them a proper burial at sea, also known as my sock pile. I then moved on to the last frontier of fighting boredom: my father's room.

I liked to jump on my father's king size bed and pretend I was one of those high flyers you see jumping off trampolines, *flying through hoops, flames lapping at my gem encrusted costume as I flip over making the perfect landing balanced on the back of a horse galloping around the big top, the crowd GOING WILD!*

I was laying with my head hanging off the end of the bed, soaking up the applause, when I noticed the corner of a dark green box poking it's head out from under my father's sheets. I felt it my responsibility, as the head of the secret security force, to check this unattended package for any bombs. *We would not want any explosions ruining these people's good time, now would we?* I slowly edged the suspicious package out from under the bed using my father's back scratcher, using its little bent fingers to slowly lift the lid.

My heart stopped for a minute when I first caught sight of my Grandfather's Wampum belt. I had not seen the belt since my father moved us away from the reservation when I was just a little kid. I can still remember sitting next to Grandpa, as he would tell me stories of our people and the story of the Wampum belt.

"The two row Wampum belt represents an agreement between the Haudenosaunee, called Iroquois by Europeans, and the European Colonist," Grandpa would explain. "Although the agreement is several hundred years old it is still important today." He would point at the belt, "These two purple lines symbolize two paths or two ships. One is the path or way of the Haudenosaunee. The other, the path or way of the European." I could still hear the almost hushed tone in his voice as he continued, "Each group has its own laws, beliefs, and way of life. The belt teaches that each should travel side by side but without interfering in the lives of the other. In this way the two groups can continue to coexist in mutual respect and harmony."

I was just about to reach out and touch Grandpa's belt when I heard the front doorknob shake, and the rattle of dad's keys. I threw the lid on the box and shoved it back under the bed. I had no time to make sure it was in the exact same place, but it was going to have to do. I jumped off the bed, gave it a quick swipe to try to smooth out the wrinkles I had made with my high-flying show, ran out of the room, and dove into dad's armchair. Surely dad had heard me stomping across the floor, but I slumped down and tried to look as casual as possible as I heard the door swing open.

Dad walked in and looked at me. I stretched out my arms and let out a loud yawn, "Oh hi Dad, how you doing?"

He looked at me and you could tell he was hardly fooled and less than amused by my little stretch and yawn act. "I am doing fine, Trae. What have you been up to?"

"You know, just playing with my soldiers, fighting the Forlorn. Someone has to keep them from colonizing my sock pile."

He stared at me with that long look that all parents have that says, "If I could, I would melt your face right now and see the lies you are hiding behind those pretty little eyes of yours." I tried not to crack or show any fear under the pressure of the interrogator's bare bulb. I was sure he could see the beads of sweat gathering on my forehead. Just as I thought I was going to break, his cell phone rang, his steely stare broke, and I was free.

When he answered his phone, I swung my head towards the window and was shocked by the inky darkness outside. I had not realized so much time had passed. I could still see the rain streaming down the windows, but night had definitely snuck up on me while I had my back turned.

Dad had gone into his room, but I could still hear him talking. "I don't know, I try but I can't seem to ever get through to him. He lives in his own strange little world." The door swung closed and then all I could hear was mumble, mumble.

Talk about living in your own little world, I thought to myself. I decided to stay curled up in the chair and stare out at the darkness for a while, maybe see if dad came back out of his room. I fell asleep waiting and had more strange dreams. I kept dreaming about those eyes, the same eyes as before staring out at me.

CHAPTER SEVEN

WHEN I WOKE UP IN THE morning my wet clothing was gone, and dad's heavy sweater was tucked in tight around me. I sat there for the longest time not wanting to disturb the perfect little pocket of warmth. The clouds had broken but it still looked cold and gloomy outside in the early morning sunlight.

I could hear dad banging around in his room, probably getting ready to go to work again. He never really stopped working. After a while his door swung open and he stood in the doorway looking at me, "Come on boy, get up and throw some clothes on. We'll go down to Murray's and get a bagel before I have to head off to work."

I was a little suspicious, seeing as we hadn't gotten a bagel or anything else since who knows when, but I have to say I was pretty dang hungry after last night's show. I had fallen asleep before eating dinner, so I decided to play along for now.

Down on the street dad hailed a cab, we hopped in and were off. I don't know if you have ever been in a New York City cab, but it is a bit like getting shot out of a cannon onto the tracks of the wildest roller coaster you have ever been on. I dug my nails deep into the black vinyl seat as the cabby slung around a delivery truck and squeezed through a space not big enough for a mouse, somehow managing to miss a pedestrian who dove into the gutter to avoid the hurtling missile that was us.

"There is nothing like staring death in the face to really get those stomach juices flowing and ready for breakfast," Dad said with a rare smile as we stepped out of the cab, the driver giving a little grunt of disapproval before launching off into the abyss of swirling cars and brake lights.

We swung the old wood door with the big glass window open and stepped into the bagel shop. Of course, Murray's is not just any bagel shop, it is The Bagel Shop. They make the bagels fresh every morning and pile them high in the glass display case, right there under your nose and just out of reach of your drooling taste buds.

I loved sitting at one of the high bar tables along the wall. The wall was always covered with brilliantly colored fliers of adventure and festivals. The flier hanging above my seat offered, "A place where your imagination will sore! The Big Apple Circus with spirited horses, ferocious dogs, audacious acrobats, comical conjurors, and a singing ringmaster!"

"What more could a growing boy want?" I bellowed without even thinking.

Dad looked at me rather amused as the people sitting behind us laughed. I have to admit I was a little embarrassed, I did not realize I had said that out loud. I tried to play it off as a joke. "How dumb do they think kids are? Kids aren't going to fall for that."

Dad gave me a strange Frankenstein attempt at a reassuring smile before changing the subject, "So, your Aunt Ashley tells me you went to see your cousin at his work yesterday?"

"Yeah, so?"

"You know I don't like you hanging around those places, Trae." You could tell dad was trying to control his frustration, but really not doing so well.

"We just went to lunch."

"You know I don't like your cousin filling your head with all those stories Trae."

"The stories of our people, Dad? Your story?"

"Look Trae, you need to stay away from there and that's it!" Dad said, his anger now on full display. The people behind us shifted in their seats uncomfortably, "Your imagination runs wild as it is. I don't need him filling your head with fantastical stories."

"What if they are more than just stories?"

"This is what I am talking about Trae! Enough is enough." Dad said. "Look Trae I don't want to argue about it," he sighed. "It's over. Let's just enjoy our breakfast."

We enjoyed an uncomfortable silence over the rest of our breakfast before Dad pointed me in the direction of the subway and disappeared into a cab to speed off to his office.

CHAPTER EIGHT

I SAW THE JEFFERSON MARKET Library as I was walking towards the subway and decided I needed to go check it out again. I had only been in it once before but remembered it being a funky old building. It was a fire station back when it was first built; it had been converted into a courthouse and jail before finally becoming a library. It had a tall tower where the fireman would keep watch for fires high above the street. Inside the tower was the best spiral staircase leading down to the basement where they kept the murderous criminals during trial. It's one of those staircases right out of castle movies with the stone steps and narrow stained-glass windows casting eerie light.

I, of course, went straight to the staircase when I got there and ran up and down a few times, until I thought I was going to pass out. I went down into the basement where the cells now imprison the reference collection.

I ran my finger across the large format photography books and onto the mythology reference books until my finger came to a stop on "The Illustrated Encyclopedia of World Mythology."

It was a really big book, I almost dropped it on the floor as I pulled it off the shelf. I waddled over and dropped it on one of the big tables with a loud thump that startled me and got a rousing collective groan out of the old men sitting around reading their three-day-old newspapers.

I flipped through the colorful pages of fantastic creatures like

Pegasus, the winged horse; Indra, Hindu's mighty lord of the thunderbolt; and Osiris, the Egyptian god of air and earth. My heart almost stopped when I came across the section called "The Little People." I turned to the first page, which was a story of the Brownies, the little people of Scotland, invisible to unbelieving adults but visible to innocent children. Maybe that was my problem, I am not that innocent. The next page was the Pookas, evil little Irish spirits that appear as wild, dark horses with yellow eyes.

I turned the page again and found myself staring at a familiar looking face. It looked like the face from the bushes with its big, round, brown eyes. The description told the same story as Asija had told me about their living in caves and their love for drumming. They are believed to be kindhearted with a gentle nature but typically do not like to be disturbed. The encyclopedia also talked about there being three kinds of little people: the Rock, the Laurel, and the Dogwood.

The Rock people practice "getting even." They steal children and other things, but they only do this because their land was invaded. The Laurel people play tricks and are mischievous. They are humorous and enjoy sharing joy with others, which is why you will sometimes find children laughing in their sleep. The Dogwood people are good and take care of people.

The book says there are a lot of stories and legends about the little people. It told the story of a small boy, called the Forever Boy, who never wanted to grow up and would always go off and play by himself.

One day his father finally got tired of the games and said, "Forever Boy, I will never call you that again because you will learn to be a man. You are going to stop playing and take responsibility for yourself." Forever Boy was so broken-hearted he went out into the forest by the stream and cried and cried, he did not want to grow up. He cried so hard he did not even notice his animal friends gathering around him. They were trying to tell him something; they were trying to comfort him. Finally, he thought he heard them say, "Come here early tomorrow morning."

He thought they just wanted him to come back so they could tell him goodbye, so he dragged his feet all the way home. He could not sleep at all that night he was so upset. The next morning, heavy hearted he went out early to meet his friends as promised. He was so sad he could not hear them trying to tell him something else. Finally, he heard them say, "Look behind you."

He looked timidly over his shoulder and there they were, the little people. They were smiling and laughing as they ran to hug him. They said "Forever Boy you never have to grow up, you can stay with us forever. You can come with us and never have to grow up. We will send a vision to your parents letting them know you are safely with us." This was the last anyone has ever seen of Forever Boy to this day.[4]

I don't know about you, but these types of stories always get my spidey senses tingling and I start thinking I see glimpses of little people all over. I explored the alcoves of the basement and trudged to the top of the spiral stairs searching every crevice and hiding spot until I was too tired to take another step. I flopped down in a hard, purple plastic chair in the children's library and flipped through a toddler's bird picture book to distract my brain.

Finally, I left, my brain still seeing things everywhere, and took the subway home. I was too tired to go back to the park and look for the little people. I wandered around the apartment and flipped channels on the TV. I spun in dad's computer chair until I had to go throw-up in the garbage shoot in the hallway. I even went down and helped Eddy sort mail I was so bored. Eventually I fall asleep face down on the carpet watching episodes of some old army show.

I dreamed all night about the Forever Boy running around playing tricks on people. I dreamed I was one of the little people running around playing pranks on people with Forever Boy. At one point I crawled under Marcus's desk at school and tied both of his shoe laces to his desk. When he stood up to go home the desk flipped completely over and everything including his Collector's Edition Forlorn Action Figures, that he would not let anyone touch, went flying all over the floor. Everyone laughed and laughed at him, but he did not know how it happened. He stumbled and crawled out of the room with the desk still tied to one of his shoes. That was a good dream.

CHAPTER NINE

I WOKE UP THE NEXT MORNING face down in a puddle of drool, still laughing. "Ah crap, I got to go to school!" I said as I jumped to my feet, almost falling down because my legs had not woken up yet. *"Not so funny now, is it?"* I thought as I laughed at myself. I got dressed in a flash, ran out the door, and down into the subway. As I listened to the subway screech around a corner, I thought about how funny it was that on the days when I wasn't supposed to be to school, I was early and every time I was supposed to be at school I was always late.

I rang the buzzer and there was Mr. Johns to greet me. Off we went to the time out room for breakfast before class. It felt strangely good to be back at school where things almost felt normal. As normal as being stuffed in a desk and talked at all day can feel, that is.

"So Trae, how was your weekend? Did you do anything fun?" Mr. Johns asked.

I was too embarrassed to tell him I had shown up to school on Saturday, I mean how needy can you look? "No, nothing."

"I took my kids up to the zoo over the weekend. They love the big cats at Tiger Mountain."

Knowing Mr. Johns had kids made me kind of mad. I didn't like the idea of sharing him.

"You guys are going bowling over at Chelsea Piers today for gym," Mr. Johns said. I gave him a frustrated shrug.

"Come on Trae, it will be fun. I'm coming with you. You and I can walk over to the river, what do you say?"

"Sure, Mr. Johns," I said, with as much apathy as I could muster. I really hate bowling, but it distracted me from being mad about having to share him.

The morning passed listening to Ms. Schultz blather on and on about some old dead author or another. She tried to explain why we should care but mostly it sounded like one of those old Charlie Brown specials when the teacher talks and all you hear is wha, wha, wha, wha, wha.

I was not going to waste a whole morning though, so I got into a satisfying spitball war with Marcus. It was a very efficient use of my math homework, except for those few shots that missed Marcus and were now clinging precariously to the window.

Despite my best efforts to divert time, gym class came anyway. Gym always started the same way, all of us sitting on the floor staring up at the coach barking at us. Don't get me wrong, I love a good spit bath from a wrinkly old white guy who used to be somebody, but this guy was particularly sloppy.

Once we finished our shower, coach teamed us up with walking buddies. Of course, I got paired with Mr. Johns as my partner. For some strange reason they didn't trust me to walk with one of the other kids. As we headed out, the thick smell of grease was everywhere, and you could hear trains screeching along the subway tracks below.

Chelsea Piers, for all practical intents and purposes, is really nothing more than a giant warehouse with docks attached. No matter what time of year or time of day there always seems to be a massive wind driving through the outer shell of the building. The bowling alley was this high priced looking joint, with fancy velvet couches and dim lighting. It was all meant to make it look swanky. I don't understand why not being able to pay to light your store means high-end fancy, but it seems to be true of a lot of places.

All the kids had to find a seat on the couches before the coach would pay and then start taking kids to get their shoes one at a time. This process always takes longer than the actual bowling seems to ever last. Waiting around for everyone to get shoes is usually the point where I end up in trouble—I just don't like waiting.

As we sat there my mind kept racing back to Asija and the library. I was getting pretty tired of thinking about these stupid little people, but I could not seem to shake it. Shake something, now there is an idea. Mr. Johns must have noticed my legs starting to bounce as I began looking around for someone or something to distract myself with.

"Hey Trae, how about you and I take that walk?" Mr. Johns asked.

I jumped not realizing he had sneaked up on me while I was lost in thought. This seems to happen a lot. *I need to work on my early warning system*, I thought to myself, which made me chuckle a little. I am kind of a funny guy. Mr. Johns took my hand and pulled me to my feet.

"Come on little man, let's get out of here for a few minutes while they get organized."

Little man, I thought, *that's a strange thing to say.* I am not that little, well not for eigth grade anyway. Why would he say that? *Did I mention my mind was racing?*

We walked down past the golf driving range, with its towering black nets on one side and the glistening yachts on the other. We sat on the bench at the end of the pier and looked out over the Hudson, neither one of us really saying much, just chilling. I watched as the sail boats weaved in and out of the tugboats and mammoth cargo ships. The wind that blows down the Hudson drowns out a lot of the other noise of the city, it even managed to drown out my racing thoughts for a while.

"All right Trae, we need to go back."

"Come on, Mr. Johns, just a few more minutes?"

"We need to go, Trae."

If it would have been anyone else, I think I might have run away but I just couldn't do that to Mr. Johns, he was the only adult that ever actually seemed interested. There are those like my aunt who liked to feign sympathy for me since my mom died. Then there are those who think if they are nice to me, they can get favors out of my father. Mr. Johns was different, he seemed interested in me because of me.

Mr. Johns let us take the long way back around the pier, I think he secretly did not like bowling so much either. As we were heading back I noticed a strange, out of place boat floating between all the sailboats, motorboats, yachts, and cargo ships. It was a small, white stone canoe. Seated towards the back was a very stoic looking man with braided black hair that almost touched the water. I did not see any paddles or an engine. The boat seemed to be moving under some mystic power. I paused to watch the canoe as it was heading down the river out towards the bay and the open sea beyond.

"Come on Trae, keep moving."

"Do you see that canoe?"

"What canoe? I don't see a canoe just someone that does not want to go bowling." Mr. Johns said.

"No really Mr. Johns, there is a canoe over there."

Mr. Johns looked back over his shoulder at the river and said, "Let's go Trae. We need to get back."

We walked back in silence; I think Mr. Johns was annoyed. I was disappointed we could not stay and watch the canoe, but I was more mad than anything that he thought I was lying to him. We went back and bowled but even if my heart had been in it before, it sure wasn't anymore. Mr. Johns tried to make small talk on the walk back to the school, but I was not really interested in talking. I just wanted to get back and get this day over with.

I walked into class still steaming over what happened on the pier. Ms. Schultz smiled at me hesitantly, which was the last straw.

I could not take anymore. I flipped two of the front desks over and shoved all the papers off the top of the file cabinet. When Mr. Corfa came to get me, I had no fight left and just walked out and up to the time out room with him close behind. I sat quietly in the corner the rest of the day ignoring anyone that tried to talk to me. As soon as the bell sounded, I bolted for the front door before Mr. Johns could get to his usual spot.

It felt good to be outside and away from that stinking school. I am not sure where I thought I was going at first, I was simply happy to be going. By the time I calmed down enough to think about what I wanted to do I was already at Columbus Circle and almost home. You know Columbus—the guy that came to America and discovered we were already here.

CHAPTER TEN

I WENT STRAIGHT HOME, content to go in and try to get my broken game controller to work enough to kill a few Forlorn. When I reached the door, I dug around in my pockets for my keys but only found a crumpled up ticket from the bowling alley. I flopped my butt onto the floor and leaned back, gently banging my head on the door for a while, trying to figure out what to do. There was no way I was going to get in on my own and I did not want to admit to Eddy that I had locked myself out again.

I finally decided to just give up for now and head over to the park. At least I could be outside instead of sitting in the stupid hallway. I walked around for a while, first to the merry-go-round then over to watch some people playing baseball. I wandered until I finally found myself back at the black rock outcropping. I climbed to the top and found a good place to sit and enjoy the view. It was pretty fun just people watching.

People do the funniest things when they think no one is looking. I watched an old man in a full suit and tie picking his nose and a rollerblading lady fall on her face. Then I began to hear the soft beat of drums coming from the bushes below. At first, I wanted to ignore them, it seemed that all that nonsense had caused me nothing but trouble lately. My dad is mad at me, Mr. Johns is mad at me, and I couldn't seem to keep my head straight. I knew everyone else thought I was crazy, and lately I was starting to agree with them.

The drums kept getting louder and louder but no one else

seemed to even notice them. I started back down the rock. I just wanted to get out of there, it was starting to make me nuts. By the time I reached the bottom the drums filled my head and I could not hear anything else. I started walking towards home not really sure how I was going to get in, not really sure I cared. As I got further from the rock the drums did not seem to fade but instead grew louder and louder. I got more and more frustrated and angry. I wanted to turn around and go back to face my tormentor, after all I had never run from a fight before.

When I got to the edge of the park and was about to round the wall I finally broke. I turned and started straight back towards the bushes, I was determined to settle this thing once and for all. Either there was going to be something there or there wasn't, but this was it. I literally dove into the bushes headfirst, fully expecting to find nothing but a bunch of discarded wrappers.

I was shocked when I found myself face to face with a pair of beautiful brown eyes. I scrambled back on my hands and knees. I shook my head trying to erase the image like my eyes might be some kind of weird etch-a-sketch. When I looked back to where I had seen the eyes, there was a little person standing just outside the clump of bushes staring at me. She was draped in a beautiful deerskin dress with colorful beading. She did not seem shocked or scared—which was all right, seeing as I was shocked and scared enough for the both of us.

I jumped to my feet as she stood quietly smiling at me. As I started to slowly walk towards her, I realized she was no longer so little. It took a minute to sink in that she had not grown but everything else around me had. I looked up at the towering bushes that just a minute ago came to my waist and the Monolithic rock outcropping that now seemed to go on forever.

The girl turned and started to walk back into the bushes looking over her shoulder at me as if to urge me to follow. I hurried after her, but she stayed just far enough ahead that I could only catch glimpses of her.

Eventually I lost sight of her all together. I stumbled around in the thick brush until suddenly breaking into a clearing. I found myself looking out over a wide valley with several streams coursing through it. The streams spilled into a large lake with several islands covered in thick pine trees. Along the edge of one of the streams was a grouping of thatched buildings irregularly circled around a central courtyard. Across from the village was a large forest. The girl was standing next to me, seeming to appear out of nowhere.

She glided gracefully down the steep embankment with me close in tow, trying not to stumble and fall over myself as I tried to take it all in. We circled down into a small clearing among the stand of old growth trees with their big gnarly branches and thick coat of leaves. At the edge of the clearing a couple of people sat playing instruments while a cluster of people danced about in the center of the clearing, seemingly unaware that we were even there.

The girl began to swing her arms and kick her feet, twirling in circles to join the other dancers. I watched, mesmerized by all the action. One musician tapped a rattle made of two beautiful turtle shells against his leg, the other musician beat joyfully on his drum creating the prefect rhythm for dancing. The musicians and dancers all looked so carefree and happy. Soon the girl that brought me twirled out to where I was watching and took my hand and led me gracefully into the middle of the circle. She took my hands and swung our arms from side to side over our heads and spun us around. At first I tried to struggle against her, nearly stepping on her toes a few times. I finally just gave in and let myself go. I danced around flinging my arms wildly until the music finally stopped and I fell to the ground gasping for air and laughing like I had not laughed since before mom died, since before dad made us leave the reservation.

The girl came over and helped me to my feet as the other people walked off into the woods and disappeared. She led me back the way we had come, away from the others.

"Who are you?" I asked excitedly "What is this place?"

She looked back at me as we continued to walk, "So many questions Trae. Enjoy the now."

I paused, almost pulling our hands apart, "Do I know you?"

She did not answer but instead began to tell me about the drums, "The skin of the drums reminds us to respect the animals. The wooden base of the drum reminds the people to respect the plants and trees. The water in the drum reminds the people that we need water to live. The round shape reminds the people of the circle of life. The beat of the drum reminds us of our heartbeat and to cherish the gift of life."

I could not stand it anymore, "Why are you telling me this? Why won't you answer my questions?"

"Come Trae, we must hurry back."

"Back? I don't want to leave yet! I want to dance some more before we go!"

"You will come back but for now you must go," she said as she took her hand from mine and pointed back through the bushes.

I turned and she was gone. I found myself lying right where I had landed, everything exactly as it had been except that night had fallen and the park was nearly empty. I laid there for a while in shock, which slowly gave way to disbelief and then a sense of feeling really silly. *Obviously I had fallen asleep right? That could not have really just happened, could it?* The thought that she was not real and that none of that had happened was just too sad to consider.

I knew there would not be anything there, but I had to look anyway, so I dug back into the bushes before standing up and brushing myself off. I wandered out of the bushes and walked along the dimly lit paths towards my apartment building, lost in the rhythm of the music still running through my head. As I swung the door open to the lobby Eddy looked startled to see me standing there.

"What are you doing out alone this late at night?"

"I'm locked out of my apartment."

"How long have you been locked out?" Eddy said with a serious sound of concern in his voice.

"Since school got out."

"Why didn't you come and find me Trae?" he said, "You cannot be running around by yourself all day and night."

I was not sure how to respond, I was kind of shocked he was talking to me like I was his own son.

"I just picked up this ham and cheese down at the deli, you sit here and eat while I go and get the key to let you in," he continued.

I wanted to yell at him that he was not my father and walk away but I had nowhere to go. Besides, the thought of sitting down seemed surprisingly good. I jumped up on his stool and peeled back the aluminum foil. The steam rose from the meat as the cheese dripped down into the foil.

I had not realized how hungry I was until I started eating and the hot juices began dripping down my chin. I was so caught up in the sweet ham and cheese goodness of my sandwich I had not even noticed that Eddy had returned and was watching me with deep concern.

"Where have you been since school Trae?"

"The park."

"You spent all this time at the park? What were you doing?"

I was still trying to figure that out myself and Eddy's questions were starting to really irritate me.

"Just playin'," I said, trying to hide my growing irritation. After all, the guy just fed me.

"All right, I'll leave you alone," Eddy said with a little smile. I knew there was a reason I kind of liked this guy.

Eddy let me into the apartment and as soon as the door closed behind me, I ran over to the window and looked down at the park. I knew I wouldn't see anything but I still had to look. I stared out the window for a while at the lights in the park until my eyes would not stay open any longer. I wandered into my bedroom, kicked off my shoes and crawled into bed.

43

CHAPTER ELEVEN

I DREAMED THAT I WAS STARING out the window at the park and a large black raven landed on our ledge in front of me. He sat staring at me with one big round black eye before jerking his head around and staring at me with the other. He seemed to be studying me for something but what for I have no clue. After several minutes of this stare down, the raven turned and with a single flap of his wings vanished into the darkness.

The alarm scared me so bad I jumped, landing on my feet on the bed; well momentarily anyway, I hit the bed so hard I bounced backwards and banged my head on the wall. Dad must have come in after I was asleep and set my alarm. I never set it and I don't know why he thought he needed to do it.

I stumbled around the apartment for a while, hardly able to keep my eyes open. I had not slept at all well, thanks to the strange dreams. My head felt like a giant bowling ball trying to topple over onto the floor. Somehow I still managed to get dressed and stumble out the door, making sure I had my keys this time.

I walked down to the subway and hopped on the downtown train towards school. I usually don't sit down but today even the short ride to school seemed too much to take. The cool, hard seats actually seemed to help my thumping headache and before I knew it, I was off to dreamland again. I would have ended up out in Far Rockaway had some old goat in a suit not kicked me as he was trying to get off the train. By then I had already missed my stop, but a least

I could get off before crossing under the river into Brooklyn. I fumbled around for my backpack and got off the train just before the doors mashed my brains in.

Still not really awake I staggered over to the other platform and caught the train back, this time standing up.

Of course, by the time I got to school I was late. Mr. Johns greeted me at the door as usual, taking me straight to the timeout room. Once I sat down, I faded into a fog. The last thing I remembered was seeing Mr. Johns walk out. I awoke to Mr. Corfu shaking me. "Get up Trae. Your father is on the phone."

"Yeah hello." I said

"What's wrong with you boy? I set the alarm for you so this wouldn't happen anymore."

I was still a bit groggy and disoriented, "Yeah dad."

"'Yeah dad?' I get pulled out of meetings and you give me 'yeah dad'?"

"Sorry dad?"

"Eddy told me you came stumbling in well after dark last night. Tonight after school I want you to go straight home; no detours, no leaving the house again. You hear me?"

"Sure dad." I was too tired to fight and not sure I really wanted to do anything but go home and sleep anyway.

I hung up the phone and Mr. Johns led me down to the second floor kitchen to dig out a carton of milk and a muffin before leading me off to class.

"You all right Trae? You seem really tired today."

"Bad dreams that's all. I'm fine."

"All right little man. Are you going to be able to stay awake?"

"I think so." Besides what choice did I have?

I wolfed down my muffin and milk before walking into class. Ms. Schultz gave me a concerned smile and waved me to my desk. The class was right in the middle of our quiet reading time. I pulled out my book and laid my head down across my arm as I read.

The next thing I knew, Ms. Schultz was standing over me "Trae, Trae, time to wake up. It's gym time, let's go." I looked up my eyes still full of blur. The classroom was empty except for the two of us. I could hear my classmates out in the hallway, shouting at each other to get in line and laughing. She led me out to the hallway where we stood at the back of the line, waiting for the gym coach to lead us up. That's one thing I didn't like about this place. Get in trouble a couple of times, get transferred to a school for "problem students," and all of a sudden, they don't even trust you to walk down the hall by yourself.

Ms. Schultz walked beside me all the way to the gym and led me over to the bench to sit with her while the rest of the class went and sat on the floor. "Are you all right Trae? Do you think you are ready to join the rest of your class?"

I gave a halfhearted nod, not sure I wanted to do anything but sleep some more. She gripped my hand and led me out onto the floor where everyone was lining up for dodge ball. We leaned back against the wall waiting for coach to yell "Go!" at which point everyone is supposed to rush for the balls on the center line and begin trying to hit the people on the other side. Normally I am the fastest one on the court and can collect a couple of the balls before anyone else gets there to challenge me—usually—but today coach yelled go and my body said, "Yeah right, I don't think so." While everyone else was running around chasing down balls, my sorry little butt stayed planted against the wall. The funniest part about the whole thing is I ended up being one of the last three people left before someone on the other team accidentally hit me while trying to get one of my teammates.

After gym was lunch, which we had in the gym so we did not have to go anywhere so I could just leave my butt planted right where it was. By the time lunch was over I was finally starting to feel awake, and by the end of the day when the bell rang, I felt ready to roll, until I remembered my conversation with my dad.

When I got home, I flopped down on my bed and stared at the

ceiling for a while, hoping to fall asleep again; but the more I laid there, the more my mind raced. I could not stop thinking about yesterday and the girl from the bush; the rhythm of the drum.

I finally could not stand laying there any longer and went out to play video games. The stupid controller was still broken and every time I would try to sniper one of the Forlorn from my perch, I would drop my rifle and switch to fist. How exactly I was supposed to punch someone from 300 yards away I am not sure—but the game seemed convinced I should try.

CHAPTER TWELVE

I EVENTUALLY GAVE UP TRYING to sniper punch Forlorn and decided to go jump on my Dad's bed again. As I walked into his room, I remembered the green box and Grandfather's belt. I scurried under the bed, pulled the box out and opened it carefully. The smell of Grandpa's house rose out of the box and I could see Grandpa's warm, wrinkly, old face staring down at me as he told me stories about the animals.

It was in the fall when leaves are yellow that it happened, and long, long ago, he would start. *The buckdeer were coming down from the high ridges to visit friends in the lowlands along the streams as they have always done. The Duck-people had gathered to go away. The old man could see the Duck-people on the lake getting ready to go away, and at that time they all looked alike; that is, they all wore the same colored clothes. The loons and the geese and the ducks were there and playing in the sunlight. The loons were laughing loudly.*

On the hill where the old man stood there was a great deal of moss, and he began to tear it from the ground and roll it into a great ball. When he had gathered all he needed he shouldered the load and started for the shore of the lake, staggering under the weight of the great burden. The Duck-people saw him coming with his load of moss and began to swim away from the shore.

"Wait my brothers," he called. "I have a big load here and I am going to give you people a dance. Come help me get things ready."

The Gray goose said, "Don't you do it, that old man is up to no good. I just know it."

The loon called out and told the old man they would not help at all. Right near the water the old man dropped his ball of moss and then cut twenty long poles. He used the poles to build a lodge that he covered with the moss, leaving a doorway facing the lake.

Inside the lodge he built a bright fire and cried out, "Say, brothers, why should you treat me this way when I am here to give you a big dance? Come into the lodge!" But they would not go in. Finally, the old man began to sing a song in the duck-talk, keeping time with his drum. The Duck-people liked the music, and swam a little nearer to the shore, watching for trouble all the time. But the old man sang so sweetly that pretty soon they waddled up to the lodge and went inside. The loon stopped near the door, for he believed that what the gray goose had said was true, and that the old man was up to some mischief. The gray goose too was careful, but the ducks went all around the fire.

"This will be the Blind Dance," the old man said, "but first you will have to be painted."

"Brother Mallard, name the colors—tell how you want me to paint you."

"Well," replied the mallard drake, "paint my head green, and put a white circle around my throat, like a necklace. I want a brown breast and yellow legs but don't paint my wife that way."

The old man painted him just as he asked, and his wife, too. Then the teal and the wood duck and the spoonbill and the blue bill and the canvasback and the goose and the loon—all chose their paint. The old man painted them all just as they wanted him to, and he kept singing the whole time. They looked very pretty in the light of the fire.

"Now," said the old man, "as this is the Blind Dance, when I beat upon my drum you must all shut your eyes tight and circle around the fire as I sing. Everyone that peeks will have sore eyes forever."

Around the fire they came with their eyes still shut, and as fast as they reached the old man, the rascal would seize them, and wring their necks. Ho! things were going fine for the old man, but the loon peeked a little, and saw what was going on; several others heard the fluttering and opened their eyes, too. The loon cried out, "He's killing us—let us fly," and they did. There was a great squawking and quacking and fluttering as the Duck-people escaped from the lodge. Ho! but the old man was angry, and he kicked the back of the loon-duck, and that is why the loon's feet turn out from his body when he tries to stand.

And all of the Duck-people that peeked that night at the dance still have sore eyes—just as the old man told them they would have. Of course they hurt and smart no more, but they stay red to pay for peeking and always will. You have seen the mallard and the rest of the Duck-people. You can see that the colors the old man painted so long ago are still bright and handsome, and they stay that way forever and ever.[5]

Grandpa would lean back at this point and stare off into the sky with a look on his face like he was pleased by his story. Now, of course, it was not his story; it was the story of our ancestors, but I loved hearing it just the same and never got tired of it.

I took out Grandpa's belt and spread it across my waist as I laid back on dad's bed and stared at the ceiling the way grandpa would stare at the sky. I was rather pleased with myself that I could remember so much of the story.

I don't remember much about the reservation. I was only six when dad and I moved to the city after mom's death. I remember the Bear Den restaurant near the edge of the small town we lived in. It had red vinyl booths with crusty looking fake flowers down the dividing wall. Mom and I would share the Papa Bear breakfast with ham, sausage, bacon and THREE eggs! I always wanted to order my own, but mom would always say, "Well, momma is not that hungry. Can she just share a little bit of yours?" I would always tell her there wouldn't be enough if we shared but we always had lots of extra. I could smell the bacon steaming up and see the runny yellow yokes circling around the plate. Mom would sometimes let me order a side of pumpkin pancakes and I loved to flood the plate with the warm maple syrup.

I could feel myself starting to drift off to sleep, so I put Grandpa's belt back in the box and shoved it back under the bed. I decided to lie back on dad's bed just for a minute. Big mistake. The next thing I remember is waking up in my own bed wrapped up in my dad's blanket with the alarm blaring at me. I shuffled around the apartment for a few minutes trying to get my brain to wake up. I stepped on one of my old green army guys, which not only helped wake me up it gave me a chance to let out a string of words I am not sure I realized I even knew.

CHAPTER THIRTEEN

I FINISHED GETTING READY for school and headed out, but not before giving my green army man, now freed from his base, a swift kick across the room. Somehow, I actually made it to school on time and got to eat breakfast with everyone else, which you would think is a good thing, but it was school and it's me. I was sitting at the table minding my own business, I know it's hard to believe, when an orange smacked me in the back of the head. Everyone started laughing as Mr. Johns yelled out, "Who did that?"

Everyone froze except Marcus who kept laughing and said, "It looks like he is going to cry." I picked up my carton of milk and threw it, hitting Marcus square in the face. The carton exploded, sending milk flying everywhere and left Marcus dripping. Marcus jumped over his table and came straight at me. The next thing I knew, Marcus and I where rolling around under the table punching and kicking at each other.

I could hear Mr. Johns and the rest of the staff yelling at the other kids to get back as they all laughed and screamed. I felt a strong hand reach in and grab the back of my shirt and pull me out. I went sliding across the floor almost crashing into the wall. The hand briefly let go then grabbed me under the armpits and lifted me to my feet. By the time I got my head back I was almost to the time out room. Ms. Gramber, one of the other crisis workers dragged me into the time out room and glared at me with complete disdain.

"Ms. Gramber, get out here and help get these kids back in their classrooms, now!" I heard Mr. Johns snap. Ms. Gramber held her cold stare on me as she went out the door.

A few minutes later, Mr. Johns came back and took me to the counselors' office. He closed the door and slowly circled the desk without looking at me. He reached over, picked up the phone just looking at the dialing pad. "What am I supposed to do Trae?" Mr. Johns said with a sadness I had never heard before in his voice. "I want to help you, but I don't know how to get through to you."

He stared at the phone and did not look at me. I had never felt so low in my life. I did not like the feeling. I did not like disappointing Mr. Johns, even though I seemed to do it a lot. We sat in really uncomfortable silence for what seemed like a month. My mind raced from one excuse to the next, trying to figure out what I should say or do to make this nasty feeling go away.

Mr. Corfa came in, mercifully breaking the silence just before my brain would have exploded out of my head and run off across the floor. "I think we need some help cleaning up this mess. Come on Trae, you have a lot of work ahead of you."

Mr. Johns gave Mr. Corfa a small nod but did not look up. I wished he would just look up and let loose on me with his rage. I kept wishing he would yell at me or at least look at me. Please yell at me, don't just sit there and look sad.

I was actually relieved to be on my hands and knees with milk dripping on my head as I mopped up. At least I did not have to see Mr. Johns sitting there staring at the phone with that sad disappointed look on his face. *Who does he think he is anyway?* I don't care what he thinks; he's nobody. I cursed his very existence under my breath, but it did not make me feel any less miserable.

It seemed like every time I would get a puddle cleaned up, I would turn around and there would be another puddle waiting. I spent the rest of the day mopping up puddles and sulking over spilled milk. The truth is, I probably could have been done sooner but I was afraid of having to face Mr. Johns again. I was afraid he was going to turn my feet out and make me blind for not listening. All right not really, but it would have actually been easier than the guilt trip he laid on me.

When I went down to the front door after the bell rang, Mr. Johns was not there. I was relieved and disappointed at the same time. As I was walking away, I looked into the principal's office where there was a big meeting going on. I could see Mr. Johns sitting and listening. My heart sank. I had broken the one person that actually seemed to believe in me.

CHAPTER FOURTEEN

I WANDERED OVER TO THE PARK and into the bushes, not sure what I was really planning, just knowing I wanted to get away. I sat down in the bushes and began to think about Mr. Johns. I did not notice the young girl from the other day as she approached me and gently touched my arm. I pulled back startled, but she just smiled. "Come with me, I have been waiting for you," she said in a gentle voice. I followed her but my head was nowhere to be found, it kept drifting back to earlier today. We wandered down through the trees where we had danced and into the valley below. We stopped at a small group of kids playing a game I had never seen before. I kind of half–heartedly watched as they played. All the kids would hide kernels of corn in one hand. One of the kids would throw eight dice with his other hand. The winner would get some of the hidden corn kernels. If the person with the dice dropped one while shaking them, they would lose their turn. The game continued on this way with everyone laughing and talking excitedly until a girl with a green ribbon in her hair had all the corn. Her hand was so full you could see the corn bulging out between her fingers.

When the game was over they divided all the corn back out evenly between them and ran back to the village leaving me and the girl alone. She got up and motioned me to follow her back towards the trees.

"What is wrong with you today Trae? You seem so sad," she said.

"I am sad."

"But why?"

"I disappointed a friend today. I let him down." *Did I just call Mr. Johns a friend?* That's strange.

"Ah, that is good."

"It's good that I let my friend down?" I asked angrily.

She just smiled, "No, it is good that you feel sad for doing so. It means you are almost ready."

"Ready for what?" I said, but somehow she managed to pull another disappearing act and I was alone in the bushes talking to myself, yet again. I really hated that. I decided to soothe my frustration by rescuing a hot dog from a boiling doom in the seething underbelly of the nearest hot dog cart.

When I got home dad was already there, which rarely happens. As usual, when it did happen, he was not alone. A few of his friends from work liked to come over and drink expensive wine and smoke smelly cigars out on our tiny little balcony. They seemed to think it made them bigger than life. I went in and quickly got ready for bed before going out and giving my dad a hug. He looked rather shocked at first when I hugged him, but then pulled me in close and whispered, "Good night Trae, sleep well son." There was a certain kindness in his voice that I was not used to hearing anymore but I kind of liked it, in a manly way of course.

It took a while to get to sleep, my mind would not stop racing. I don't know how many soldiers I counted that night, but man, sleep was not my friend. When I did finally get to sleep, I had wicked bad dreams about Mr. Johns. I kept dreaming I walked into the time out room and he was standing there with his back to me, so I tried to go around to stand in front of him but no matter how fast I ran his back was always turned towards me. I know it doesn't sound like much, I mean there was no slasher music or anything, but it was really creepy.

When I woke up the next morning, I was super tired, but I dragged myself out of bed determined to get to school on time—I was not about to face the wrath of Mr. Johns in my sleep again.

When I got to school I went straight to our class's table for breakfast, avoiding direct contact with as many people as I could.

Marcus kept trying to get my attention and when that did not work started trying to get everyone else to get my attention, no doubt to get into mischief together again, but I was determined not to go there. *Did I mention I was still a little freaked out by my dream?* I managed to get hit with just about everything but the chair I was sitting on by Marcus and some of the other kids at his table.

When breakfast was mercifully over, I cleaned up around myself and shuffled off to class. Ms. Schultz started class by reading to us for a half hour. She said it was to "bring us into the room." I think it was meant to put us to sleep. Today she was reading from some old English guy's story about dreams in the summer or something. I have to admit though her voice was very soothing as she rattled on:

This is a story by William Shakespeare called A Midsummer Nights Dream. In this story there is a wood spirit named Puck, who creates all types of mischief and mayhem. We meet Puck in scene two when Titania comes across him.

TITANIA: Either I mistake your shape and making quite, Or else you are that shrewd and knavish sprite Call'd Robin Goodfellow: are not you he That frights the maidens of the villagery; Skim milk, and sometimes labour in the quern And bootless make the breathless housewife churn; And sometime make the drink to bear no barm; Mislead night-wanderers, laughing at their harm? Those that Hobgoblin call you and sweet Puck, You do their work, and they shall have good luck: Are not you he?

PUCK: Thou speak'st aright; I am that merry wanderer of the night. I jest to Oberon and make him smile When I a fat and bean-fed horse beguile, Neighing in likeness of a filly foal: And sometime lurk I in a gossip's bowl, In very likeness of a roasted crab, And when she drinks, against her lips I bob And on her wither'd dewlap pour the ale. The wisest aunt, telling the saddest tale, Sometime for three-foot

stool mistaketh me; Then slip I from her bum, down topples she, And
'tailor' cries, and falls into a cough; And then the whole quire hold
their hips and laugh, And waxen in their mirth and neeze and swear
A merrier hour was never wasted there.[6]

Ah, the story of me and my friends, both old and new. "Listen to
me, I think I am a character out of that old English guy's story now."
I said louder than I thought and started to laugh.

Ms. Schultz looked up from her book as everyone started
laughing. I put my head down on my desk not sure what else to do.
I listened to Ms. Schultz continue to drone on in the strange
language that almost sounded like English until I finally fell asleep.

I woke up to a small puddle of drool and an empty classroom.
This seems like it is becoming a habit, young man, I thought to
myself with a little smile. What was strange though, was that the
lights were off, and no one was in the room, not even Ms. Schultz.

I wandered out into the hallway and could hear my class in the
computer lab laughing and talking really loudly. I pushed the door
open and Ms. Schultz just looked up and smiled, "Have a good nap?
Maybe if you were not out making mischief all night Mr. Robin
Goodfellow, you could stay awake during my class." I sat down next
to her, behind the other students. She gave me a warm look and
pulled me in for a big old side hug. I cuddled up next to her with her
arm around me and we just sat there watching the rest of the class. It
was really strange but nice. It's the first time I had really felt safe since
mom died. *I mentioned it was strange right?*

After computer lab we had prize closet, which I always miss out
on because I can never seem to get any points, go figure. When the
bell rang, I walked out kind of half wanting to see Mr. Johns, kind
of half afraid to. As I walked towards the door he stepped out of the
principal's office and looked at me uncomfortably.

"Hey Mr. Trae, can I talk to you for a minute?"

"Sure Mr. Johns," I said nervously. I knew I had not done
anything wrong, but when you are in trouble as much as I am, you're

always racking your brain trying to figure out if there was something you forgot you did.

We stepped into an empty room. As Mr. Johns sat down, he looked me in the eye and said, "Look Trae I should have never said what I said to you yesterday. I care about you very much and sometimes I forget you're just a little boy. I really want to help you and I feel like yesterday I kind of let you down."

I was stunned and not sure what to even say, so I just stood there staring at him. "I'm sorry Mr. Johns."

"For what son? You didn't do anything wrong."

"You always trust me, and I always let you down." I could feel my guts coming up, they wanted to come right out through my nose. I don't like that feeling.

"I think maybe we let each other down yesterday Trae. Here is the thing: I don't expect you to be perfect. I know we are going to have ups and downs, but you have to hang in and work with me, alright?" He held out his fist for a fist bump. I reached up, thumped him on the fist, and walked out feeling like total dirt.

I went straight to the park and climbed to the top of the rock outcropping. I inched my way to the edge and stared down at the bushes below. I just wanted to jump in the bushes and disappear forever into that other world. I had not felt this crappy since the funeral, and I wanted it out of me. I decided to climb back down and walk home.

CHAPTER FIFTEEN

I GOT INSIDE AND LOOKED AROUND for something, anything to distract myself but nothing looked like any fun. I went and sat on my dad's bed. I stared at the wall racking my brain for something to distract myself. I decided to pull out the green box thinking maybe playing with Grandpa's belt would distract me.

I pulled out the belt and stood up to wrap it around my waist, but when I looked down, I noticed a small piece of paper that was stuck in one of the corners of the box. I reached down and tried to pull it out without tearing it. I was finally able to work it loose and turn it over. It was a picture of mom in her dancing dress with me clinging to her side in my little buckskins.

I remembered this picture, I remembered that day at the powwow. It was right before mom got too sick to get out of bed, about two months before she died. I sat on dad's bed and stared at the picture studying every curve and crease of her beautiful, gentle face. I had not seen a picture of her since we moved from home; I thought dad left them behind with the rest of our life.

"What are you doing Trae, have you lost what little sense you have?" I must have been really deep in thought because I had not even noticed my father walk in. He was standing in his doorway with a gray face and eyes that looked like they where going to pop. "You have no right to be... Get out!"

I ran out of the room and dad slammed the door behind me. I was in shock. How did he get in without me hearing him? How did he...?

Why...? How dare he?! *Not real coherent but I was in shock, alright?* I went into the bathroom and sat on the toilet not sure what else to do.

I could hear dad through the wall, banging around for a few minutes. When the banging stopped, I could hear my dad crying. I don't remember ever seeing or hearing my dad cry before, not even at mom's funeral. I was shocked and a little scared. I leaned up against the wall and listened to him crying for I don't know how long. I heard his cracking voice say, "I am so sorry baby. I am trying to do the best I can, but I can't do it without you. He needs his mom. I need you."

I sat there listening, unable to move until my legs finally went numb, which kind of has a way of snapping you back to reality. I stumbled into my bedroom and slipped into bed as quietly as I could. I did not want to attract any more attention to myself, I had broken enough people for one day.

I dreamed all night of dancing with my mom during the powwow, bells tinkling and beads sparkling on her dress. I dreamed about her picking me up and spinning me around as the drums pounded like the heartbeat of the earth. I dreamed about sitting on our blanket on the grass, eating and laughing.

I got mad when I woke up in the morning, so I tried to fall back to sleep. I kept flipping over, hoping to drift back to sleep; I did not want to leave my dream. I finally gave up and went out into the living room. Dad's door was still closed, which seemed strange. He was usually awake long before me and sometimes not even home.

I watched cartoons for a while, played with my army guys, and stared out the window waiting to see if dad would come out of his room, but he never came out. I went into the bathroom and pressed my ear up against the wall, but I still couldn't hear a thing.

I could not take the tension anymore and decided to go outside and play. Maybe the sun would make the gross feeling in my guts from the last two days go away. I wandered around the park and ended up in a small group of trees overlooking the lake. I sat down, picked up a stick, and started digging down though the leaves and into the dirt. I was looking down at the hole I was digging flinging dirt down the hill when I got that strange feeling that I was being watched again.

The girl from the bushes was standing next to the tree in front of me. "Hello Trae," she said as she began to walk towards me. She reached out, grabbed my hand, and gently pulled me to my feet. We walked down through the trees and suddenly I found myself standing at the edge of the small village I had seen from the distance when I had been with her before.

"Come on Trae. I have someone I want you to meet"

"But I don't even know who you are yet."

"I am Ela," she said without stopping to look back at me.

We walked into the village where the longhouses were sitting in a scattered circle. We went to one off to the side. It was made of bark and branches. Other than the bright red carpet acting as a door it did not stand out from the rest. Ela pulled back the rug covering the entrance and waved me in. Inside was an arrangement of beds and an area for cooking and eating, simple but inviting. Sitting on the end of one of the beds was a small, young-looking man with long black braids. He looked up, smiled a big warm smile, and waved Ela and I over to join him.

"Ela has told tales of your recent adventures Trae. You must be tired and a bit confused, but do not worry—with time things will become clear. You carry much sadness with you today." I looked down at my feet, kind of ashamed and angry that my pain was so obvious even to a stranger. I kicked at a small pile of dirt, making a puff of dust.

"It is all right to miss your mother Trae."

He caught me by surprise. I looked up, shocked at this strange man. "What do you know about my mother?" I said, with more anger in my voice than I expected to hear. Embarrassed by my outburst, I stared back down at my feet.

"I know the pain of death and loss Trae; we all do since Coyote brought death to the people."

"Brought death to the people?" I said, trying to steady the shaky anger in my voice.

"Sit Trae, I will tell you of Coyote," He waved me towards the blanket before continuing.

In the beginning, death did not exist. Everyone stayed alive until there were so many people that there wasn't room for anyone else. The chiefs held a council to determine what to do. One man arose and said that it would be good to have the people die and be gone for a little while, and then to return. As soon as he sat down Coyote jumped up and said that people ought to die forever because there was not enough food or room for everyone to live forever. The other men objected, saying that there would be no more happiness in the world if their loved ones died forever.

All except Coyote decided to have the people die and be gone only for a little while, and then to come back to life.

After the council, the medicine men built a large grass house facing the east. They gathered the men of the tribe and told them that the people who died would come to the medicine house and then be restored to life. The chief medicine man said that he would put a large white and black eagle feather on top of the grass house. When the feather became bloody and fell over, the people would know that someone had died. Then all of the medicine men would come to the grass house and sing a song that would call the spirit of the dead to the grass house. When the spirit came to the house, they would restore it to life again. All of the people were glad about these rules regarding death, for they were afraid for the dead.

One day they saw the eagle feather turn bloody and fall and they knew that someone had died. The medicine men assembled in the grass house and sang for the spirit of the dead to come to them. In about ten days a whirlwind blew from the west, circled the grass house, and finally entered through the entrance in the east. From the whirlwind appeared a handsome young man. All of the people saw him and rejoiced except Coyote, who was displeased because his ideas were not carried out.

Shortly thereafter the feather became bloody and fell again.

Coyote saw it and at once went to the grass house. He took his seat near the door and sat with the singers for many days. When at last he heard the whirlwind coming he closed the door before it could enter. The spirit in the whirlwind passed on by.

This is how Coyote introduced the idea of permanent death, and people from that time on grieved about the dead and were unhappy. Now whenever someone meets a whirlwind or hears the wind whistle they say, "There is someone wandering about." Ever since Coyote closed the door, the spirits of the dead have wandered over the earth, trying to find some place to go, until at last they find the road to the spirit land.

After that day, Coyote ran away and never came back for he was afraid of what he had done. He always looks first over one shoulder then the other, afraid that someone is pursuing him.[7]

"It's alright to be sad Trae. It is alright to miss your mom and your past." Ela said in a low gentle voice, "Come, we must go."

"Why? Why do I have to go?" I tried to shout but I was so tired it barely came out a whisper.

"There is much you must do but the time has not yet come."

I didn't want to leave, but I could tell fighting wouldn't get me anywhere, besides I was too dang tired to argue anymore.

Ela led me out through the trees to the spot overlooking the lake before disappearing behind a large, knotted tree. I sat watching parents wandering through the park, kids close in tow. I watched this mind numbingly drab scene as I thought about how much I missed my mom. The pain felt like a heavy rock sitting on my chest. I wanted to cry but the tears would not come.

After a while I gathered enough steam to move. I wanted to see my cousin again. I know dad told me to stay away, but I really wanted to talk with someone who would remember the same things I remembered from home.

CHAPTER SIXTEEN

I RODE THE SUBWAY DOWN TO the construction site and waited outside the gate for Asija to finish work. I didn't know what time it was or when he got off work, but I really didn't care—I was going to wait.

I played with the bags of toys hanging on the outside trellis at the small bodega by the gate. They always had the strangest things: brightly colored Chinese dragons, umbrellas, GI Joe knock offs, plastic cars, and a few other random things for lost tourists to throw in their bags and take home. I was so caught up in looking at all the stuff I almost missed Asija as he walked out and started down the street.

"Hey, Asija, wait for me!" I yelled, running after him.

"What's up, Trae! What are you doing here?"

"I, uh, just wanted to hang out."

"I thought your dad didn't want you hanging out with me anymore?" He said, suddenly making me uncomfortable.

"I know, but...."

"Come on Trae. We can walk to the subway together, but then you better head back home. Your dad is not going to be happy with either of us."

"So how is work going?" I said, desperately trying to keep from getting blown off.

"Why do I get the feeling you did not come all the way down here to ask me about work?"

I paused, a little embarrassed and kind of pissed off frankly, "Can't I just want to see my cousin?"

"Is that what's really going on, or is something else on your mind?"

"Do you remember the reservation?"

"Sure, why?"

"I have just been thinking a lot about it and about mom."

"Ah, I see," Asija said. "Do you remember when you and your mom would come and watch me play lacrosse?"

My mom and I would go down to the high school every Saturday and watch him play lacrosse for the team. Lacrosse was actually invented by the Native Americans, not many people know that. I remember Asija always seeming larger than life when he played, he seemed to be a whole head taller and much faster than everyone else. We talked about some of his best moments and victories on the field as we walked towards the tunnels. The pain of missing mom faded away and it almost felt like we were back in those better times.

When we reached the subway platform, I knew it was time for us to go our separate ways, but I really didn't want to go home. We talked as I waited with Asija for his train. When it came, he jumped on and waved goodbye. As I started walking down the platform, I heard the bell ringing for the doors to close, and, at the last second, decided to dive into a car a couple down from Asija's. I hoped I could remember which stop was his, though I was not really sure what I was going to do when we got there. Jump out and yell "Surprise!" maybe?

After we crossed under the river into Brooklyn, I started poking my head out at every stop—watching to see if he got off. After about four stops, I finally saw Asija walk out onto the platform and start for the stairs. I jumped out and started running after him. He must have heard me running because he stopped and looked over his shoulder to see what was going on. He looked really shocked and unsure what to say. I had not figured out what to say yet either, so we just stood there staring at each other.

Asija finally let out a heavy sigh and said, "Alright. Let's go to my house and you can join us for supper before I take you home."

I followed quietly behind him. We walked through the brownstone row houses and apartments with their fancy black railings, and flowers and fake birds spilling out of overstuffed pots. I had only been here once before when my father and I came to bring some things to his sister after we first moved from the reservation. My father refused to come to Brooklyn after that; he seemed to think it was beneath him. I did not recognize Asija's apartment building until he started up the stairs. It was an unassuming brownstone in a long row of unassuming brownstones.

When we walked into his apartment, the sights and smells of Grandma's old house hit me. The apartment was filled with blankets, rugs, fancy bead works, and drying spices from the reservation. It was like stepping back in time. I loved it, I felt like I was home. I heard my Aunt in the kitchen cooking. She called out to Asija, "You hungry boy?"

"Yeah mom, but I have a guest that wants to see you."

"Someone wants to see me?" she said as she walked into the living room. She stopped dead in her tracks when she saw me standing there staring at her with a silly smile on my face. I was so happy I could not get rid of it.

"Trae! It's so good to see you! What are you doing here?"

My heart sank a little as the reality that I was a long way from my home on the reservation sank in. "He followed me home on the train and I could hardly just leave him standing on the platform." Asija said.

"Well, your father is going to be beside himself," she said.

He won't even notice I am missing, I thought.

"Let's give him a call, then you both better sit down and help me eat all this food."

She slipped into the bedroom and I could hear her calling my father. I was shocked that he actually answered the phone. I could hear my aunt talking but couldn't really make out what she was saying. She finally came into the kitchen and dished up our plates while we sat down.

"Your father is not pleased Trae. He says you have been gone since before he got up this morning. What have you been doing?"

"I'm surprised he even noticed I was gone; he doesn't usually even know I exist." I said without thinking.

My Aunt got a sad look on her face, "He knows. He just has no idea how to talk to you. He loves you very much."

"Yeah, I don't know about that." I said with a twinge of anger that seemed to catch my Aunt off guard.

"He does Trae, I know he loves you. It has not been easy for him since your mom died."

"Tell me about it! It has not exactly been fun for me either, you know!" I could feel myself getting red.

My Aunt looked like she was about to break into tears. *I have a great effect on adults lately, don't I?* "I think sometimes we forget how hard this all must have been on you. You are just a kid; you had no control over any of this." She said, as tears started streaming down her face. I felt like a real jerk. "It's not fair Trae. You shouldn't have had to lose your mom and get ripped from your roots that way."

I had this burning feeling that I needed to fix things for my aunt, I needed to do something to make her feel better. "Ah, I'm fine. I'm sorry for what I said, I didn't mean it."

She looked at me with a deep sadness that made me want to start crying too, but I was determined not to give in. She pulled me close and cried. I could feel her warm tears dripping down on my head. I could feel tears starting to well up in my eyes. After a while she pulled back, wiped away her tears, and said, "Alright then, that's enough of that. We need to finish our dinner."

We ate the rest of our dinner in an uncomfortable silence, the type of silence I had gotten used to with my father. After dinner we cleared the plates and moved into the living room where my Aunt had a stack of photo books sitting on the coffee table.

"Come sit down Trae," she said, "I will have Asija take you home in a little bit but come sit for a while."

We flipped through the photo albums talking about the reservation and the different trips and adventures we all had. We talked about mom and dad, but we talked about the good memories, how much she loved us, not about her sickness or the pain. We talked about the super yummy food we used to all make together when we would have barbeques.

My Aunt told me the story my mother used to always tell me when I would get into mischief. It was a story about a silly boy who wanted to learn magic. The story goes that Veeho is like some tourists who come into an Indian village not knowing how to behave or what to do, trying to impress everybody.

One day Veeho met a medicine man with great powers. This man thought to amuse Veeho with a little trick. "Eyeballs!" he shouted, "I command you to fly out of my head and hang on that tree over there." At once his eyeballs shot out of his head and in a flash, they were hanging from a tree branch. Veeho watched open-mouthed. "Ho! Eyeballs!" cried the medicine man, "now come back where you ought to be."

"Uncle," said Veeho to the medicine man, "please give me a little of your power so that I too can do this wonderful trick." Veeho was thinking to himself, "Then I can set up as a medicine man; people will look up to me and give me many gifts."

"Why not?" said the medicine man. "Why not give you a little power to please you? But listen, Veeho, don't do this trick more than four times a day, or your eyeballs won't come back."

"I won't," said Veeho.

Veeho could hardly wait to get away and try out this stunning trick. As soon as he was alone, he ordered: "Eyeballs, hop on that ledge over there. Jump to it!" And the eyeballs did.

Veeho couldn't see a thing. "Quickly, eyeballs, back into your sockets!" The eyeballs obeyed. Boy, oh boy, *Veeho said to himself,* what a big man I am. Powerful, really powerful. *Soon he saw another tree, "Eyeballs, up into that tree, quick!" For a second time the eyeballs did as they were told. "Back into the skull!" Veeho shouted, snapping his fingers. And once more the eyeballs jumped back. Veeho was enjoying himself, getting used to this marvelous trick. He couldn't stop. Twice more he performed it. "Well, that's it for today, " he said.*

Later he came to a big village and wanted to impress the people with his powers. "Would you believe it, cousins," he told them, "I can make my eyeballs jump out of my head, fly over to that tree, hang themselves from a branch, and come back when I tell them." The people, of course, didn't believe him; they laughed. Veeho became terribly angry. "It's true! It's true!" he cried. "You stupid people, I can do it!"

"Show us," the people said.

"How often have I done this trick?" Veeho tried to remember. Four times? No, no. The first time was only for practice; it doesn't count. I can still show these dummies something. *He commanded, "Eyeballs, hang yourself on a branch of that tree!" The eyeballs did, and a great cry of wonder and astonishment went up. "There, you louts, didn't I tell you?" said Veeho, strutting around and puffing himself up. After a while he said: "Alright, eyeballs, come back!" But the eyeballs stayed up in the tree. "Come back, come back, you no-good eyeballs!" Veeho cried repeatedly, but the eyeballs stayed put. Finally, a big fat crow landed on the tree and gobbled them up.*

"Mm, good," said the crow, "very tasty." The people laughed at Veeho, shook their heads, and went away.

Veeho was blind now. He didn't know what to do. He groped through the forest. He stumbled. He ran into trees. He sat down by a stone and cried. He heard a squeaking sound. It was a mouse calling out to other mice. "Mouse, little mouse," cried Veeho, "I am blind. Please lend me one of your eyes so that I can see again."

"My eyes are tiny," answered the mouse, "much too tiny. What good would one of them do you? It wouldn't fit." But Veeho begged so pitifully that the mouse finally gave him an eye, saying: "I guess I can get along with the other one."

So Veeho had one eye, but it was exceedingly small indeed. What he saw was just a tiny speck of light. Still, it was better than nothing.

Veeho staggered on and met a buffalo. "Buffalo brother," he begged, "I have to get along with just this tiny mouse eye. How can a big man like me make do with that? Have pity on me, brother, and lend me one of your big, beautiful eyes."

"What good would one of my eyes do you?" asked the buffalo. "It's much too big for your eye hole." But Veeho wept until the buffalo said: "Well, alright, I'll let you have one. I can't stand listening to you carry on like that. I guess I can get by with one eye."

And so Veeho had his second eye.

The buffalo's eye was much too big. It stuck out of its socket like a shiny ball that boys like to play with. It made everything look twice as big as his own eyes had. And since the mouse eye saw things ten times smaller, Veeho got a bad headache. But what could he do? It was better than being blind. "It's a bad mess, though," said Veeho.

Veeho went back to his wife and lodge. His wife looked at him. "I believe your eyes are a little mismatched," she told him. And he described all that had happened to him. "You know," she said, "I think you should stop fooling around, trying to impress people with your tricks."

"I guess so," said Veeho.[8]

We totally lost track of time until the dog came in the room, begging to be taken for his late-night walk.

"It's after 10:00. Your father is going to be freaking out."

Doubtful I thought, but I did not want to upset my Aunt again, so I kept it to myself.

"I will call your father. Asija, take him home in a cab and make sure he gets there safely, you hear me?"

"Of course mom," Asija said, a bit irritated by the idea he would not make sure I was safe.

Now I have already told you about the wild rollercoaster ride that is a New York City cab ride, but let me tell you, by the time we got to my house I thought I was going to hurl everywhere.

Asija delivered me to the apartment door, wobbly legs and all, where I let myself in before he left. When I got inside, I was surprised to see my father sitting in his armchair looking out over the park.

"Hello Trae," he said in a low soft voice. "How was your Aunt's house? She still make a pretty good pot of spaghetti?"

It was strange, but it seemed like he was really just kind of talking to fill up the space and not really sure what to do. "Yeah, I guess it's pretty good."

"Alright son, why don't you go off to bed. I will see you in the morning." And that was it.

I did not realize how freaking tired I was. I had not been home all day and all of a sudden it hit me; I could hardly keep my eyes open. It had felt good to be at my Aunt's house and to feel normal for a little while, but now I was ready to just be home. I got undressed, climbed into bed, and was out almost right away.

"Do you know why cricket is black, Trae?" My mom asked, standing over me as I knelt in our front yard. I looked at her through the sunglasses she had bought me for my fifth birthday party. The sun directly behind her made her look like one of those silhouette dolls.

"Cricket and Mosquito were going to have a feast," she said. "So Cricket sent Mosquito to catch some eels while he built a fire. Mosquito came back and Cricket asked how many eels he had

caught. Mosquito said that he had caught one eel the size of his leg. Cricket thought this was awfully funny and laughed so hard that he fell into the fire and got burned. That is why the cricket is black."[9]

I looked down at the cricket in my hand and smiled. "So mister, you're that color because you were too busy making fun of your friend. Silly man." My mom used to always call me silly man when I would laugh and giggle, which was most of the time when I was little.

I woke up giggling and wanted to fall right back to sleep before the dream was gone, but I was too late. I sat on the bed thinking about all the pictures we looked at last night and the fun times we used to have before everything went bad.

CHAPTER SEVENTEEN

DAD CAME INTO MY ROOM dressed in jeans, a T-shirt, and a ball cap—not exactly dad's normal uniform. "Come on Trae, it's time to get going. We are going to be late."

"Late for what?"

"Don't you worry about that, just get ready," I had not seen dad this excited for a long time. It was really strange, but I decided to get up and get ready. When I walked out into the front room dad was drinking his coffee. He gulped down the last of it, handed me my game boy and said, "let's go!"

We took the cross-town bus to Grand Central Station. I loved going into Grand Central Station's main concourse and seeing the sky ceiling: sparkling gold stars and lights shining against a dark blue sky. It was huge and always made me feel like I was standing in the middle of outer space.

Dad stopped by the Hudson News stand before we headed down and jumped on the number four uptown train. We sat down next to each other as the train rattled off into the tunnels, him reading his newspaper, me playing a game. I lost track of time while we were down in the tunnels, too caught up in my game to even wonder where we were going anymore.

We hopped off the train at 161st street. "So Trae, how about you and I go to a Yankees' game?" I am not a baseball fan, but I have to admit getting to go to a Yankees' game with my dad sounded kind of cool.

"Alright," I said as calmly as I could, knowing my excitement was showing, as we walked towards the huge stadium. The growing crowd of people was buzzing. When we got inside, we wandered around looking at the different stands with hats and foam fingers. We walked past the food stands: Carvel's Ice Cream, Famiglia Pizza, and Nathan's Hot Dogs. I had not realized how hungry I was until we started passing them. After doing a full lap dad finally turned in to the line for Nathan's Hot Dogs. I got a really large lemonade and a dog with just mustard. Dad got his loaded down and got us a big box of Red Vines. Dad seemed determined to do this baseball thing right.

Our hands were overflowing as we made our way to our seats along the first base line. I started laughing as dad fumbled all his food when the guy asked for our tickets so he could show us where to sit. Dad shot me a look when I started laughing—it was a cross between frustration, embarrassment, and wanting to burst out laughing himself.

We downed our hotdogs and ate a few of the red vines while we waited for the game to start. We did not talk a lot, but it was fun just being there with my dad. After a while dad went back to reading his paper and I watched the players warm up and stretch. Dad did not really come back from the world news until the end of the second inning when he folded up his paper and stuck it under his seat.

I really did not understand a lot of what was going on and started to get bored. Dad must have noticed because he tried to explain who all the different people were, but I heard a lot of blah, blah, blah then a loud roar as the crowd reacted. I decided every time other people would scream and cheer I would too. Dad would yell, "What's wrong with you? Are you blind or something?" So I would yell, "Yeah, you blind or what?" *Keep in mind I didn't even know who I was yelling at.* The one I really liked and actually got was when the other kids would yell at the batter, "Hey batter, batter swwwwwwwing batter!" Not sure why that was so much fun, but it was.

We passed the rest of the game with dad yelling at the umpires and me trying to trick the batters into swinging at every pitch. Oh yeah, and loads of junk food. After the game we talked baseball all the way home and until dad turned my bedroom light off and shut the door.

I dreamed all night about baseball.

The next morning my alarm went off way too early. I slammed the button down and tried to rollover and go back to sleep but it was no use. I got up, got dressed, and wandered out into the front room. Dad had already left for work, his coffee cup still sitting on the counter. I was still buzzing from the game as I left for school. As I walked to the subway I would pretend to step up to the plate, knock the dirt out of my cleats with my bat, stare down the shaking pitcher, and of course hit one out of the park. The crowd roared as I rounded the bases. I did this all the way to school not really caring who noticed me: after all, I was the greatest hitter of all time.

During breakfast I talked with Mr. Corfa and one of the eighth-grade teachers, Mr. Parker, about baseball. They kept talking about ERAs and the batting averages of all the players for the Yankees. I did not understand what they were saying but kept right in the middle of the conversation anyway, talking a hundred miles an hour about all the cool stuff that happened the day before.

During class I spent most of my time playing a game of baseball inside my desk with my erasers until Ms. Schultz called on me to read. I, of course, had no idea where we were so I just picked a random spot and started reading, which always got a laugh from the class. During lunch I rushed through eating and got permission to go to Mr. Johns and Mr. Corfa's office, where we talked baseball and football until after the bell rang. I wanted to stay in the thick of the conversation but Mr. Johns finally said, "Alright Trae, I really like seeing you happy and not in trouble, but I have to take you back to class." I tried to distract him with more baseball talk, but he took my hand and back to class I went.

At the end of the day Mr. Johns greeted me at the door with a big smile on his face, "You know Trae, it has been three or four days in a row that you have not ended up in my office because you were in trouble." He gave me a big fist bump. "I like it when you can stop by and talk sports instead of trouble. Keep it up."

I left feeling good and pretty full of myself. I was a big shot. I was on the ins with Mr. Johns and Mr. Corfa. I decided to go home, pour myself a big glass of milk and eat Oreo cookies until I got sick. After all, I earned it. After downing more cookies then is ever advisable and groaning for about twenty minutes in dad's chair, I decided to go down to the park and play. I went to Strawberry Fields. I liked to watch the tourists snap pictures of each other and to listen to the street performers as they played old Beatles' music.

CHAPTER EIGHTEEN

I WATCHED THE PEOPLE ANGLING to get the best view only to have someone step in front of them just as they took the shot. People were tripping over each other with their overstuffed camera bags, which was funny. I got bored after a while and decided to wander into the trees and hunt for the Forlorn. As I turned past the hill, I caught sight of Ela sneaking up behind a giant looking squirrel, pulling back her small bow, and taking aim. The arrow flew well over the squirrel and landed in the bushes in front of it. I started laughing at the lousy shot. Ela turned around and gave me a stern look of disapproval. She pulled out another arrow and pointed it at me, letting it fly almost instantly. It hit me square in the chest sending me back on my hind side.

"Hey, what gives!" I yelled. "You trying to kill me or what?"

Ela started laughing and pointed at my chest, covered with a purplish liquid that had splattered all down to my pants. "It's a bog berry shot. I think you might live."

"Why are you shooting berries at squirrels?"

"I am not shooting at the squirrels! I don't want to hurt them, just practice."

"You are a strange girl sometimes Ela," I said as I stood up and dusted myself off.

"Don't you ever like pretending you're a brave hunter, Trae?"

"I am a fearless soldier in hunt of the Forlorn."

"Who?"

"The Forlorn, they are the bad... Ah never mind." I said, swiping my hand at the bushes.

"I like to pretend I am hunting the monster bear!" Ela said excitedly.

"Monster bear?" I said in more of a sarcastic tone than I meant to.

"Oh, yes!" she continued, without acknowledging my sarcastic tone.

A long time ago there was a Mohawk village of bark houses along the Oswego River. One day Mohawk hunters discovered the tracks of a Giant Bear. The tracks began to show up more and more. Sometimes, the tracks would circle the Mohawk village. They soon noticed the animals were all disappearing from the forests. The Mohawks knew that the Giant Bear was killing and carrying off all the animals.

Because of all of the food disappearing, great hunger and starvation came to the Mohawks. The meat racks were empty. The people were very hungry. Starvation tempted them. One of the chiefs said, "We must kill this Giant Bear who is causing all our trouble." A party of warriors set out at once in search for the bear. They soon came across his tracks in the snow. They followed the bear tracks for many days. They finally came upon the huge beast. The warriors filled the air with arrows. To the surprise and dismay of the Mohawks, the arrows failed to pierce the thick hide of the bear. Many broken arrows fell from his tough skin.

The angry bear turned and charged the hunters, who fled but were soon overtaken. Most of them were killed. Only two hunters escaped, and they returned to the village to tell the sad tale. The two hunters told the council of the Great Bear. They told them what happened to the war party.

Party after party of warriors set out to destroy the Great Bear but they always failed. There were many battles fought between the bear and the warriors. Many warriors were slain.

79

As time went on, more and more deer vanished from the forest. The smoking racks were empty. The people became very thin because of the lack of food. Starvation caused many to become sick. The people were filled with fear and their hungry bodies crept close to the fire at night. They feared the Great Bear, whose giant tracks circled their village each night. They feared to leave their village because they could hear, coming from the darkness of the forest, the loud cough of the Great Bear.

One-night three brothers each had a strange dream. Three nights in a row, they had the same vision. They dreamed they tracked and killed the Great Bear. They said, "The dream must be true."

So, they took their weapons and scanty supply of food and set out after the bear. After a little while, they came upon the tracks of the great beast. Quickly, they followed the trail, their arrows ready.

For many moons they followed the tracks of the bear across the Earth. The tracks led them to the end of the world. Looking ahead, they saw the giant beast leap from the earth into the heavens. The three hunters soon came to the jumping-off place. Without hesitation, the three of them followed the bear into the sky. There in the skies, you can see them chasing the bear during the long winter nights.

In the fall of the year, when the bear gets ready to sleep for the winter, the three hunters get near enough to shoot their arrows into his body. His dripping blood caused by the wounds from the arrows turns the autumn leaves red and yellow. But he always manages to escape from the hunter. For a time, after being wounded, he is invisible, but he always returns.[10]

She stopped and pointed at the sky that was now dark, "See there, the three hunters are still chasing the Great Bear."

At first, I was shocked by the night sky, but shock quickly turned into excitement as Ela pointed out the three hunters chasing the bear.

I hate to admit it, but she got me. It was a good story. I stood staring at the sky while Ela sat down behind me and started making more arrows for her bow.

"Hey, will you show me how to make those? I want to learn."

She motioned me over to sit by her as she whipped small pieces of string around the wooden shaft and the berry like one of those fancy magicians you see on TV waving their hands over a hat and the rabbit magically pops out.

I grabbed a shaft, string, and berry and tried to whip it around like Ela was doing with such ease and confidence. My first attempt ended up with a nice fastening of my elbow to my thumb, leaving the berry and shaft lying on the ground dejected. Let's just say my second try did not end much better.

Ela smiled, patiently handed me a string, and took another shaft and berry. She held it up for me to slowly lace my string around with her guiding me every inch of the way. We made a few more arrows before she said, "Alright that should be enough for now. Let's try them out!

She stood up and whipped her hand through the air above her and the night sky gave way to daylight.

"What the—" I exclaimed.

"Time is relative outside of that little world you exist in Trae."

She took the first arrow and aimed at the knot in a tree and let the arrow fly almost instantly. It smashed dead center in the knot spraying its juices to drip down the tree.

"Do you want a shot?"

I took the bow from Ela, confident I could hit any target; *it didn't look all that hard, pull back and let it fly right? Wrong.*

I pulled the arrow back to notch it and it fell off the riser and landed in the dirt. Second try I placed the arrow, notched it, so far so good, I pulled back the string and the arrow came unnotched and stayed right where it was, leaving me holding an empty string.

Ela smiled, trying hard to hold back a laugh, "Let me help you

Trae. Watch what I do." She slowly this time placed the arrow across the riser, notched the arrow, placed her fingers on either side, pulled back, aimed, and let it fly. Once again, she struck her target almost dead on.

"Alright Trae, place your arrow." I placed my arrow. "Notch your arrow." I notched my arrow. "Place your fingers on either side." Check. "Pull back the string." Pulling back. "Aim." Aiming, arm getting tired now. "Let it fly." Letting it fly. I released the arrow and watched as it flew high up into the branches, wildly missing the trunk of the tree completely.

Ela giggled under her breath, "Actually not so bad for you first time Trae. Try again."

I notched the arrow and pulled back the string but forgot to keep a finger out to guide the arrow across the rise, so it fell off sideways. I tried to let off the string slowly, holding onto the arrow, but as I let go it flew about five feet in front of me skidding across the ground. Yet another misfire.

I kept practicing and after a few more shots I actually started to kind of get the hang of it. I was still sending a few into the high branches of the trees, but I also managed to actually hit the trunk of a couple of trees, not always the ones I was aiming at, but some trunks. After a while we got laughing so hard I could barely pull the bow back.

"Shoot, what time is it?" I said, realizing I did not want to be late getting home since dad had promised to try to come home earlier, at least sometimes. Things were going better, and I did not want to screw it up again.

"I don't know. Time is your worry not mine." Ela said.

"I got to go. Sorry!" I dropped the bow and arrows and ran for home, not even bothering to look back. I was so caught up in getting home I barely paused as day turned into night as I busted out of the bushes.

CHAPTER NINETEEN

I GOT HOME, THREW THE DOOR open, and stepped in just as dad was putting down his bag from work. He turned and smiled at me, "I thought I had missed you. I am glad you are home."

I started pulling my shoes off when my dad interrupted me, "Do you want to go down and get some food or should we call Five Guys to bring us some burgers?"

"Five Guys!" I exclaimed. They are way good.

Dad ordered for us and we went about our own business, not really talking, but it was cool to be home with dad anyway. He sat in his chair and read his paper while I played my game. He would look over every once in a while and make a comment about what was happening in my game.

During dinner I sat on the floor next to dad's chair as we ate.

"So how was school Trae."

"Good."

"Just good? Anything else?" Dad said, with a little frustration in his voice, which made me nervous.

"It was fun."

"Fun?" Dad said suspiciously. Man, just no pleasing some people.

"I talked with Mr. Johns and Mr. Corfa about our baseball game."

Dad smiled warily, "Why were you in their office?"

"I ate lunch with them, but I wasn't in trouble."

Dad looked relieved and went back to eating his food as I chattered on about every detail of my power lunch. After dinner he went back to reading, I got ready for bed and played my game until he told me it was bedtime. It was kind of earlier than I was used to, but I did not want to argue. I laid in bed thinking about talking with the guys about baseball and trying to learn to shoot the bow until I drifted off to sleep. Notch the arrow, pull back, and swwwwwwwwiiiing batter swing.

The next day was a pretty typical morning, well until I got to school. I walked into class all happy until I found out that Ms. Schultz was not coming in and that Ms. Roffin was going to be teaching our class. Ms. Roffin was this mean old lady with thick-rimmed glasses and wiry grey witch hair. I decided to try to make the best of it since usually it meant a day of "working individually and quietly," or to put it another way, "figure it out for yourself, keep quiet, and, most importantly, leave me alone."

True to form, she walked in, handed us a stack of work sheets and a reading assignment and barked at us to "get busy." I sat quietly, kind of working on my schoolwork, kind of not, until she finally announced our first ten-minute break when we could go use the restroom or find something quiet to do at our desk.

I pulled out my notebook, tore out a bunch of pages and started wrapping them around each other and taping them to try to make a bow. I kept working for about thirty minutes when Ms. Roffin finally snapped at me to, "put those papers away and get back to work!"

During lunch she made us stay in the classroom to eat and play quietly at our desk. I pulled out my bow and continued assembling it. I got a nice long shaft and built the rise before digging through my desk and finding the broken string to my yoyo. I fastened my bowstring and made myself an arrow. It was right about then that Ms. Roffin finally looked up from her book and noticed my invention.

"What do you think you are doing?" She roared causing

everyone in the classroom to stop cold in their tracks. I did not realize she was talking to me at first but froze just the same.

"Trae! What are you doing?"

"Playing?"

She stared me down sternly before walking over, sticking her head out the door, and calling for Mr. Johns.

"Trae needs to go to time out right now, Mr. Johns."

"Alright, what did he do?" Mr. Johns said, sounding rather sad and disappointed.

"He is making weapons in the classroom! I want him suspended immediately!"

Mr. Johns stepped in with a genuinely concerned and puzzled look on his face as I stood there with a paper bow that was breaking at the seams as I squeezed it.

"Alright Mr. Trae. Let's go up stairs and figure this out."

"This is bull!" I shouted, not able to keep it in any longer.

"I know Trae, just come with me, alright? We will talk about it."

I griped the sides of my desk ready to send it flying but Mr. Johns came over and bent down and whispered in my ear. At first, I had no idea what he was saying, the only thing I could hear was my heart pounding in my ears. I finally heard him whispering, "Come on Trae you have been doing really well. Don't blow it now. We can work this out. Give me a chance alright? You're going to be alright; I promise."

I slowly let go of the desk. Mr. Johns took my hand and led me out of class. I was really pissed and did not want to look up or I might punch the first person who smiled at me. We went out into the hallway and straight up to Mr. Johns office. He waved people off that tried to talk to me on the way up, sent the students hanging out in the office back to class and closed the door.

"Are you kidding me!" he cried out, which made me jump a little, of course.

I was afraid to look up, sure that he was mad at me; I had let him down yet again. I had not noticed Mr. Corfa was in the room. "What's going on?"

"Ms. Roffin is losing her ever loving mind! She's plain nuts!" Mr. Johns said.

I glanced up shocked and more than a little confused. I must have misunderstood what Mr. Johns had just said. *He hadn't really just called a teacher nuts, had he?* I watched confused as Mr. Johns waved his arms in the air in frustration, then looked over at Mr. Corfa who looked as lost as I felt.

"She calls this a weapon," Mr. Johns continued, throwing my now mostly broken bow across the desk at Mr. Corfa, who picked it up and looked at it with confusion.

"This is a weapon?" Mr. Corfa asked no one in particular. I was still in shock, too confused and afraid to even know how to begin to answer.

"It's ridiculous," Mr. Johns said, "She thinks he needs to be suspended. It's just crazy making I tell you!"

"I don't get it," Mr. Corfa chimed in. "Am I missing something? A weapon? It is paper, right?"

I was still stunned and not sure what to say so I just sat quietly, kind of hoping they would forget I was in the room. I was afraid that in all their confusion they had forgotten to be mad at me.

Mr. Johns let out a big sigh before finally looked over at me. "I am really sorry, Trae. We should not be talking about your teacher like this. She is still your teacher and we need to be nice."

Alright, now I was really confused. He was apologizing, so was I in trouble or not? I really didn't know what was going on. Mr. Johns walked out of the office and disappeared for a while. He finally returned with the principal. They were both talking excitedly as they came into the office. I thought for a minute they had forgotten I was there, and I could maybe sneak out. The principal was upset that Mr. Johns was not supporting Ms. Roffin in her decision that I should be suspended. Mr. Johns did not seem to be backing down though.

He walked over to his desk and picked up the pieces of the bow, "With all due respect, this is a weapon, Mike? Come on, be reasonable!"

The principal looked over, somewhat surprised to see me sitting there. "Can you excuse us Trae?"

I stepped out into the hallway but I could still hear them arguing. The principal said, "I know you're right, Will, but we can't contradict each other in front of the kids."

"But what about when the adult is just plain wrong? What are we supposed to do? Suspend the kid for the adult's overreaction? How is that teaching the kid right from wrong?"

The yelling stopped and there was just silence for several moments. I started getting really nervous for Mr. Johns. Was he going to get fired because of me? Finally, the principal came walking out and motioned for me to go back into the office. I went into the room and looked at Mr. Johns, who was clearly exhausted. I felt horrible.

"Have a seat, son."

"I am sorry Mr. Johns."

"Why are you sorry Trae?"

"I didn't mean to make a weapon, well I meant to make a bow and arrow, but I didn't mean to hurt anyone, honestly," I said nervously.

"Trae you didn't do anything wrong. People around here just get really edgy when it comes to weapons in a school. They don't want to see anyone get hurt. We know you didn't mean to cause trouble. Just remember to be careful while you're here at school to not make these types of things out of paper, alright?"

"Do you have to call my dad? How long am I suspended for?"

"You're not suspended Trae. You are not in trouble. No one is calling your father."

"Wait, what?"

"It's alright," Mr. Johns smiled reassuringly.

I almost started crying. I was happy, confused, sad, embarrassed - I don't know what I was. I wanted to run over and throw my arms around Mr. Johns. He had kept his promise. But of course, I played it cool.

Mr. Johns tried to break the awkwardness, "Want to play a game of checkers?"

"I guess?" I said, still a little hazy about everything that just happened.

"You are not in time out, you're just going to hang with us until the end of the day so there is no more trouble with Ms. Roffin, alright?"

"Sure." I said, finally feeling a little relieved.

CHAPTER TWENTY

WE PLAYED A COUPLE OF GAMES of checkers with Mr. Johns trying to help me out. He tried to explain why he moved his pieces where he did and guided me where to place mine. I was having fun, but I could not shake the feeling that this was not over and that I needed to tell him and Mr. Corfa I was sorry.

While we were playing Mr. Johns asked, "So where did you get the idea to make a bow and arrow out of paper Trae? That was pretty creative."

I was scared to tell him the truth because I was afraid he would think I was crazy or something, so I just made up a story about liking to go to the park and pretend I was a warrior. I told them the tale of the monster bear but with me as a lone warrior chasing the monster bear across the night sky. They both laughed at the end of the story and asked me if I just made that story up. I told them it was an old story from home.

Mr. Corfa said, "That's a great story Trae. Did I ever tell you I fell in love with the most beautiful woman in the village?"

She had many suitors and after a while she grew tired of all our courting. So one day, she called a meeting at her house. All the suitors attended, including me.

She had recently read a book about a golden fruit that existed in mythology. In the myth the fruit grew near a cave in a forest. That day, she told all the suitors about the fruit of the Exillian tree. She told them that she would marry whomever bought her the fruit.

89

I went immediately to my home and read all about the Exillian fruit. I learned that the tree was rumored to grow in a forest, near a cave, only a few days walk from the village. I traveled for three straight days, until I finally came to the forest. I spent another day looking for the cave. Finally I found it! Next to it stood the Exillian tree, shimmering in the sun as though it was a gift from the gods.

I approached it slowly, mesmerized by the shimmering fruit. I was reaching out, just about to grab the fruit, when I heard I raspy hypnotizing voice say, "Who goesss there?" I jumped back, startled as a big green snake appeared from the mouth of the cave. The snake head was soon followed by a lion's body with a lion's head and a goat's head. I recognized the monster immediately as a Chimera.

I slowly drew out my knife and prepared for battle. The lion turned to me and spoke in a regal voice, "Beware mortal for this is where your life meets a bitter end. I will tear you apart with my claws and eat your flesh for my dinner." At this the snake looked startled and turned to face the lion, "I thought we were going to poissson him! You sssaid I would get the next victim." Then the goat head joined in, "Like, no! It was so decided that, like, I would, like, be the one to kill the next, like, victim."

"I am king! I get him!" roared the lion.

"But, like, why do you, like, get to be the king?"

"I dissstinctly remember you getting the prey lassst time, ssso it'sss my turn to feassst," hissed the snake.

"I am the lion which means I am the king and I say it's my turn!"

After several more minutes of listening to this fighting, a brilliant idea came to me. I began to slowly inch towards the tree. The three heads were too busy fighting to notice their prey was getting closer and closer to the prize. I plucked one of the golden fruits and walked away, smiling as I thought about the looks on my friends' faces when I told them how my cleverness and bravado helped me beat the ferocious chimera.[11]

"And that, my friends, is how I got my wife to marry me," he said with a big grin as he took a big bite of a golden delicious apple.

Mr. Johns gave a small chuckle and said, "That's a nice story, but let me tell you the story of a true hero."

When I was a young lad not much older than you, Trae, I would visit my grandparents in Romania during the summers.

I would spend my days walking the woods close to the village where they lived. The woods were overgrown with ivy and brambles, so I often carried my grandfather's sword with me. One day as I was hacking my way through a particularly dense bramble bush, I heard a young girl scream. Now, rumor had it that a dragon lived in these woods and would occasionally feast on lost children—so when I heard the scream, I made my way towards it as quickly as possible.

Soon I came to a clearing where a young village girl was crouched in fear before a towering dragon. I immediately drew my sword and jumped to the girl's defense.

The dragon and I battled back and forth. First one having the advantage and then the other. The clang of my sword against the dragon's claws and scales rang throughout the woods. We fought all day and into the night.

Finally, just when I thought I would have to surrender, I cornered the dragon. As I swung my sword for the dragon's neck, it cried out, "Wait!"

I paused to hear what it had to say.

"I have all the world's flies trapped in my throat. If you cut off my head, they will be free and will bother mankind with pestilence and biting," the dragon said.

"I would rather swat flies than allow you to eat innocent children!" I exclaimed as I swung a mighty blow that sent the dragon's head flying into the woods.[12]

Mr. Johns slapped his neck, "Dang flies!" We all broke out in roars of laughter.

91

We kept trading stories, as we played game after game of checkers, each story more outlandish than the last until the bell finally rang to go home.

As I got up to leave Mr. Johns stopped me and said, "Trae, I want to thank you for trusting me this morning. I am really proud of you. You have started to show a real change in your behavior." Not sure what to say I just held my fist up for a bump before leaving.

CHAPTER TWENTY-ONE

I WALKED DOWN THE STAIRS and was reaching for the classroom door so I could get my stuff when I heard Ms. Roffin arguing with who sounded like the principal.

"What are you telling me? He is not going to be suspended, he just gets to have weapons at school, and no one will do anything?"

"Of course not, don't be ridiculous."

"He had a weapon at school, and I am being ridiculous?"

At this point I started to get really uncomfortable, so I decided to just leave my jacket and get it later. I was not about to get in the middle of that. I walked really quickly to the door and out onto the street before either of them came out.

All the confidence that I had gotten talking to Mr. Johns had left my body and I just wanted to run. I was sure I was going to get in trouble when I got home so I decided to walk over to the Hudson River Parkway and take the long way. I walked down the parkway along the river, watching the boats drifting up and down, trying to get my mind to stop thinking about Ms. Roffin.

I watched the waves splash up against the banks. The water suddenly went from its usual green and healthy look to a black fiery sludge. A thick blanket of garbage and debris floated to the top. Startled, I pushed back from the rail and looked at the other people along the trail, but no one else seemed to notice what was going on. I looked back down, and the river was back to its nice healthy-looking green self. I looked as far up and down the river as I could see, trying to find the massive black slip of fire with its coat of garbage but there was no trace of it. I walked away from the river, my legs really shaky, but I did not want to sit down. I just wanted to get away from that bizarre scene as fast as I could. First the guy in the white canoe and now this, I think I have had enough of the river.

I decided I was too freaked out to just go home, if dad was there, I was sure I would get yelled at and if he wasn't there, I did not want to be in that empty apartment alone. I went to Central Park and decided to park myself somewhere. I went to the place back in the trees where Ela and I had been target practicing to see if I could see any of the juice marks we had left behind.

I was staring high up into the trees when I heard Ela behind me giggling, "Are you looking for your lost arrows, Trae?"

"Very funny Ela. What are you doing here?"

"I am out practicing and playing with my friends."

"Who?" I said looking around but seeing only Ela.

"The squirrels, silly." She said as she began to giggle again.

"Pretending to be the great hunter in search of the mighty scourge of squirrels that must be eliminated?" I said jokingly.

Ela stopped giggling and got a serious look of concern on her face.

"What's wrong Ela?"

"Why would we want to eliminate our animal friends? We need them."

"I was just teasing, Ela but do we really 'need' them?" I said a little annoyed. "Sometimes you can be a very strange girl."

"Have you ever heard the story of the buffalo from the Kiowa people, Trae?"

"No," I said still annoyed at her comment

Once, not so long ago, the buffalo were everywhere. Wherever the people were, there were the buffalo. They loved the people and the people loved the buffalo. When the people killed a buffalo, they did it with reverence. They gave thanks to the buffalo's spirit. They used every part of the buffalo they killed. The meat was their food. The skins were used for clothing and to cover their tipis. The hair stuffed their pillows and saddlebags. The sinews became their bowstrings. From the hooves, they made glue. They carried water in the bladders and stomachs. To give the buffalo honor, they painted the skull and placed it facing the rising sun.

Most of all, the buffalo was part of the Kiowa peoples of the Great Plains. A white buffalo calf must be sacrificed in the Sun Dance. The priests used parts of the buffalo to make their prayers when they healed people or sang to the powers above.

When the white man came, they were new people, as beautiful and as deadly as the black spider. They took the lands of the people. They built the railroad to cut the lands of the people in half. It made life hard for the people and so the buffalo fought the railroad. The buffalo tore up the railroad tracks; they chased away the cattle of the white man.

The buffalo loved the people and tried to protect their way of life. So the white man's army was sent to kill the buffalo, but even the soldiers could not hold the buffalo back. Then the army hired hunters. The hunters came and killed and killed. Soon the bones of the buffalo covered the land to the height of a man, sometimes for miles along the railroad tracks. The buffalo saw they could fight no longer.

One morning, a Kiowa woman whose family was running from the Army rose early from her camp deep in the hills. She went down to the spring near the mountainside to get water. She went quietly, alert for enemies. The morning mist was thick, but as she bent to fill her bucket, she saw something. It was something moving in the mist. As she watched, the mist parted and out of it came an old buffalo cow. It was one of the old buffalo women, who always led the herds. Behind her came the last few young buffalo warriors, their horns scarred from fighting, some of them wounded. Among them were some calves and young pregnant cows.

95

The woman watched as the old buffalo woman led the herd straight toward the side of the mountain. As the Kiowa woman watched, the mountain opened up in front of them and the buffalo walked into the mountain. Within the mountain, the Earth was green and new. The sun shone and the meadowlarks were singing. It was as it had been before the white man came. Then the mountain closed behind them. The buffalo were gone.[13]

"We must learn to live in harmony with our world. If we do not care for it, it will not be able to care for us. You know this already though, don't you Trae? You have begun to see the visions, haven't you?"

I was shocked and thrown off by Ela's question. Was she talking about the black tar river and the man in the white stone canoe?

"I don't know what you mean Ela." I said, afraid to answer honestly.

"It's alright Trae. They are scary, but they have a purpose and you are not alone."

"Hey kid! Throw that ball back over here, would ya?" A loud voice yelled.

I turned around and found a baseball resting in the bush. I picked it up and threw it to a tall, slender man. When I turned back around to ask Ela what she meant, she was gone and I was alone again.

I hunted around in the bushes, behind the trees, and even called out to her, but she was gone. It was really frustrating the way she would just disappear at all the wrong times. How am I supposed to get any answers if she keeps doing that? Maybe she really is just another one of my daydreams—but if she is, why can't I conjure her up anytime I want?

Tired and hungry I finally gave up and decided I could not avoid going home any longer. My stomach sank as I walked towards the apartment. I was sure that the school had called and told my dad I was suspended for making a weapon at school. I was sure he would be there waiting for me, watching and waiting. When I got into the apartment, dad was not sitting in his chair. I searched the apartment and there was no dad. I was so relieved that I just flopped down on the floor with a big sigh.

While I was lying on the floor I looked over and noticed the message light on our phone was flashing madly. So much for breathing. No one ever leaves us messages; it had to be the school. I got up and stood in front of the phone, contemplating my fate. The message surely had to be from the principal telling my father that I was a total demon child and to never send me back to their school.

I walked away and tried to distract myself. I played my game, turning the volume up really loud, thinking somehow the noise would drown out the flashing light, but it did not work - the light just kept mocking me. I decided to spin in my dad's chair as fast as I could for as long as I could thinking maybe I could scramble my brains into forgetting that the light was flashing. I spun and spun until I fell out of the chair onto the floor where I had been to start with and there it was, that stupid light, still flashing its mocking little self at me.

I laid there for a while considering my choices: melt into the floor, hide in my closet until I turned 18, runaway to clown school, or maybe, just maybe, I could listen to the message and delete it. Maybe my dad would never be any wiser. Besides, how much more could he do to me than he was going to if he found out I was suspended?

I picked up the phone and hit the button for messages, my stomach on the floor. "First message from phone number 646-555-0037, beeeeeeeeeeeeeeee, *annoying right?* eeeeeeeeeep. Hello Trae, this is dad. I just wanted to let you know I will be a little late getting home, so I left you a few dollars on the counter to go down and buy yourself one of those sandwiches you were telling me about—the one like you got from Eddy? Anyway, I will be home as soon as I can buddy."

That was weird. Dad had never called before. Maybe he was

setting me up, he did not want to tip me off that I was in trouble. *Knock it off Trae, you're making yourself nuts! If you don't stop, I am going to make you spin until you throw up. Don't make me do it, because you know I will!* At least I could still laugh at myself, right? I did start to feel a little relieved. Maybe Mr. Johns was right and nothing bad was going to happen.

I decided to go back to playing my game that I had not bothered turning off, so it was still blaring in the background. I played until my stomach began trying to eat itself before deciding I better get myself that sandwich. I was surprised my dad even remembered that story about Eddy giving me the sandwich when I was locked out.

I went to get my sandwich then decided to sit with Eddy in the lobby while I ate. Just like old times, I joked to myself. Eddy was in particularly good spirits for some reason and was telling me tales of his most recent bizarre adventures. I am pretty sure I should not have been listening to some of his stories at my age.

After a couple too many tales I went back upstairs and watched a PBS special on the wild hunts of the Norse. The story goes that Odin could often be heard but seldom seen in mad pursuit on his eight-legged horse across the sky. People who saw the passing hunt and mocked it were cursed and would mysteriously vanish, those that joined in the hunt were rewarded with gold.

I was almost falling asleep watching Odin race across the screen when I heard dad wiggling the doorknob as he fumbled with his keys. The sinking feeling came back as I waited for what may be my doom. Dad swung the door open and sat down his briefcase and keys before looking over at me. My heart was on the floor by this point.

"Hey Trae, I am surprised you are still awake. How did your day go?"

Was this some kind of cruel test? "It went alright?" I said hesitantly.

"I don't know how your day went, why are you asking me?" he said with a smile

"Well, I mean, it went alright."

Dad just smiled, "I am glad you are still up so I can tell you goodnight, but you look really tired pal. Maybe you should get ready for bed."

"Yeah maybe." I said, finally feeling like it was really over.

I went in my bedroom, got undressed, climbed into bed, and was out right away. I barely remember my head hitting the pillow I was so tired. Not surprisingly, I had really wacky dreams. I dreamt that Ela was chasing a herd of buffalo down the black, oily Hudson River while riding Odin's eight-legged horse, shooting her arrows with berries for tips.

CHAPTER TWENTY-TWO

THE NEXT MORNING I WOKE UP with a funky headache and my stomach felt like it was in total knots. I got up and went to school but by the time I hit the front door I could barely stand up straight anymore my stomach hurt so badly.

As soon as I walked in the door the principal stopped me. "You alright, Trae? You don't look like you're feeling too well."

"My stomach feels like it's eating itself and my head feels like a freaking bowling ball." I almost cried.

"Let's take you into my office. We'll call your father and see if we can't send you home or maybe to the doctor." The principal led me into his office and sat me down. I started getting nervous when he picked up the phone to call my dad, was he going to tell him about yesterday?

"Hello Mr. Monique, this is Principal Hill. I am calling about your son, Trae. No sir he is not in trouble, he is actually doing quite well lately. I am calling because he showed up here not feeling very well." I could hear my father's voice but could not really make out what he was saying.

"Yes sir, let me ask Trae. Hold on for one second please." Principal Hill said before holding the phone away. "Trae do you think you need to see the doctor or are you alright to go home?"

"I just want to go home and lay down." I said, trying to stop my voice from trembling.

Principal Hill held the phone back up to his ear, "Sir, are you still there? Good. Trae would like to go home and lay down if that's alright. Does he have a way to get in?" Mumble, mumble, mumble from the other end. "We will send him in a taxi with one of our staff to make sure he gets home safely, thank you."

"Alright, Mr. Trae, let's get you home son," he said as we walked outside and he hailed a cab.

We climbed into the cab and before the door was all the way shut, we were off in a blur of yellow haze.

I stared out the window in a daze, unable to really think. I watched the cars and the people and the trees whizzing by my window. As we pulled onto Central Park West, I watched the park whirling by. The leaves began to shrivel, and the branches of the trees began to curl up and die. The dead leaves fluttered across the street like a fierce snowstorm. The cab driver kept driving as if he did not even notice the near brown out of the falling leaves. All the people walking, the other drivers and Principal Hill all seemed oblivious to what was happening around them.

The cab screeched up to the curb in front of our apartment and the cabby turned around and said, "Alright this is it," as if nothing was happening. It was actually starting to piss me off.

I climbed out of the car and looked across the street at the park. All the trees seemed to have magically returned to their normal green healthy springtime selves. There was no sign of the dead leaves on the ground or blowing in the wind. Everything seemed normal, except me of course.

"You alright, Trae?" Principal Hill asked with an overly concerned look on his face.

"Yeah I'm good, just need sleep I think."

"Do you need me to come up with you? Make sure you get settled?"

"Nah, I'm good." I said, mustering as much courage as I could and with that, off Principal Hill went in a blaze of yellow death cab.

I went into the building, trying to shake off the bizarre delusions as just being fever, but it seemed so real I could not get it out of my mind. I walked in and Eddy greeted me like nothing was going on. I had to be losing it.

I headed to the elevator and hit the button. As the elevator started up my stomach rumbled, and I almost tossed my cookies all over the fine tile floor. I shuffled my way into the apartment dropping my bag by the door and kicking my shoes halfway across the room before collapsing into dad's chair. I sat there and stared at the ceiling in a daze as the room spun. After my head finally stopped swimming enough that I did not think I was going to hurl, I dragged myself into my room and flopped into bed. I pulled the covers over my head and burrowed deep down into the sheets, trying to shut out the world.

The next thing I remember, I could hear my dad calling from the front room. I was huddled down in my little sweaty dark cave and didn't really want to poke my head out into the cold air. My dad called out again, then I could hear him opening my door.

"Hey, Trae. It's time to get up buddy. I brought you some dinner."

"Ugh."

"Come on bud. Come and eat and then you can go back to bed, alright?"

I poked my head out and my dad was standing over me with a concerned smile on his face. "You will feel better once you eat something."

I drug myself into the front room. It was already getting dark outside; I must have been asleep for hours. Dad had brought me my favorite clam chowder with a hot bacon and cheese sandwich from Hale and Hearty Soups. I did not realize how hungry I was until I started eating. The soup left a great warm, full feeling in my stomach. I was only able to eat a few bites of the sandwich, but the warm melting cheese over the crispy bacon was perfection.

Dad kept asking me questions about how I was feeling, but I mostly just kind of grunted and shrugged my shoulders, not really wanting to talk. After dinner dad asked me if I wanted to go back to my bed or make a small bed in front of the TV for a while. I decided I wanted a bed in front of the TV, so dad laid out a pile of big soft blankets and brought my pillows from my room. I burrowed down and dad turned on a movie for me. I was still feeling really gross and could not concentrate on the movie, so I mostly stared at the light from the TV flickering off the ceiling until I fell asleep again.

When I first woke up in the morning, I felt surprisingly good, but I was afraid to move. I was worried the gross would come flooding back so I laid there slowly twitching this leg, then that arm, until I had done a full systems check. Then I slowly rolled over and angled my feet out of the covers, so far so good. I decided to get up and try breakfast, which went well, so "off to school with you" as mom used to say.

I was relieved when I walked into class and Ms. Schulz was back in her usual chair. "Hello Trae, we are glad you are back. Are you feeling better?"

I shrugged my shoulders not wanting to talk about it. We spent the morning doing our math assignments before going up to art class. After lunch we had history class. Ms. Schultz talked all afternoon about the Greek gods and their crazy families with wacky superpowers. My favorite was Hades, the god of the dead, and his three headed dog, Cerberus. I really liked the story of the Trojan War and the sneaky way they got into Troy by hiding in the belly of a giant wooden horse. I thought it was crazy how the gods punished them for their arrogance when they tried to return home after sacking Troy. Overall, a good afternoon.

I decided to walk home. As I turned onto Central Park West a dead bird fell in front of me, already stiff. I bent over to take a closer look at it and noticed another fall, then another. No one else seemed to notice as they nearly stepped on the dozens of dead birds now lying on the ground. As I continued to look around to see if anyone else had noticed I caught a glimpse through the crowd of the old man who had been floating down the river in the canoe. His face was grey with a heavy sadness. When I caught his stare, he looked at the dead birds. I glanced back at the ground, but the birds were gone and when I looked back up the old man was gone too.

CHAPTER TWENTY-THREE

I WALKED QUICKLY DOWN the street towards where I had seen the old man, trying to catch sight of him but he was gone. My heart was racing as anxiety took over my brain. I hopped the fence into Central Park and headed deep into the trees, feeling like I was going to have a massive panic attack if I did not get away from all the people. I ducked behind some bushes and leaned against a tree, barely able to breathe.

I tried to control my breathing, but I was getting increasingly lightheaded. Ela, she knew about the man and the black river! I called out for Ela as I started walking through the trees and bushes looking for her. I found her by the lake, nursing a duck with a wounded wing.

"Ela, I need your help! I think I am going mad."

"Shhh, you are going to scare the duck. It must not move until I am done."

"But Ela!"

"Shhh, be still Trae."

I waited impatiently, pacing back and forth while Ela gently tended to the wounded duck. She bound its wing and sang a sweet-sounding song in a language that seemed rather familiar. After she finished her song, she nudged the duck back towards the lake, stood up, turned around, and looked at me.

"Ela, how did you know I had seen the black river and the man in the canoe? How did you know those things? Who is he?"

"What is going on Trae? You are shaking." She said with a gentleness that I had not heard in a long time.

"You tell me! Yesterday I watched as the spring trees withered and died and today birds are falling from the sky and no one seems to notice but me! Am I loosing my mind or what?" I practically shouted. I gasped for air, suddenly realizing I had not taken a breath in a while. "Look who I am asking. I am not sure you are even real. I am probably just imagining you too!"

"You are not alone Trae. There are others."

"You said that the other day. What exactly does that even mean?" I could feel my anxiety turning to frustration as my chest heaved.

Ela studied my face, searching for something. I stared back at her.

"Alright Trae, it is time."

"Time for what?"

"Sit and I will tell you." I sat down still bubbling over with anxiety.

"You are a part of the seventh generation."

"The seventh generation of what?" I said getting tired of the cryptic talk.

According to the prophecy, seven generations after contact with the Europeans the Onkwehonwe would see the day when the elm trees would die. The prophecy said that animals would be born deformed or without the proper limbs. Huge stone monsters would tear open the face of earth. The rivers would burn. The air would be so foul it would burn the eyes of man.

According to the prophecy the Onkwehonwe would see the time when the birds would fall from the sky. The fish would die in the water and man would grow ashamed of the way that he had treated mother earth.

According to the wisdom of this prophecy, men and women would one day turn to the Onkwehonwe, and particularly to the eastern door of the Confederacy, the Kanienkehaka, for both guidance and direction. It is up to the present generation of youth of the Kanienkehaka to provide leadership and example to all who have failed. The children of the Kanienkehaka are of the seventh generation; you are the seventh generation Trae.[14]

Now I knew I must be loony tunes, me responsible for something? There is no one really dumb enough to leave anything up to someone like me. "You're kidding, right?" I said as Ela smiled reassuringly at me. "I think I am cracking up. No one would be silly enough to think I could possibly provide leadership for anything. This isn't real. You are not real!"

"It's alright Trae," Ela said reassuringly.

"Really? It doesn't feel alright! Birds are falling from the sky, rivers are burning—how is this alright?"

Ela quietly watched as I went into freak-out mode, pacing back and forth nervously, muttering incoherently to myself. I would look over at her every once and a while and she would just smile. *Really? Smile? Not helpful. Then again, she is not even real. Right? Maybe I did need some of those crazy pills the school nurse kept trying to push on me. Maybe I was crazy.*

Ela waited for a break in the muttering before finally telling a story about the Bruile Sioux:

Many generations ago Iktome the Spider Man, trickster and bringer of bad news, went from village to village and from tribe to tribe. Because he is a messenger, Spider Man can speak any language he wishes, so all the tribes can understand him.

Iktome came running into the first camp, shouting: "There is a new nation coming, a new kind of man who is going to run over everything. He is like me, Iktome, a trickster, a liar. He has two long legs with which he will run over you."

Iktome called all the chiefs into counsel, and the head chief asked, "Iktome, what news do you bring from the east?"

Iktome answered: "There is a new man coming; he is clever

like me, but he has long, long legs and many new things, most of them bad. I am going to all the tribes to tell about him."

When he left, three boys followed him to see where he was going. They watched him climb to the top of a hill. There he made his body shrink into a ball, changing himself from a man into a spider. And the boys saw a silvery web against the blueness of the sky, a single strand from it led down to the hill. Iktome climbed into the web and disappeared into the clouds.

The next tribe Iktome visited were the Lakota—the Sioux nation. Two old women gathering firewood saw him standing on a butte near their village. They went home and told the chief: "We saw someone strange standing over there. He was looking at us." The chief called for two of his wakincuzas—the pipe owners, the ones-who-decide—and said: "Bring this man to me. Maybe he has a message." They escorted Iktome, now in human form, into the camp. He stretched out his hand to the west and said, "I am Iktome. I roll with the air, and I must take my message to seventy camps. This is what I have come to tell you: A sound is coming from the edge of the sea, coming from Pankeshka Hokshi Unpapi—the Shell nation. One cannot tell where this voice is coming from, but it is someplace in the east. It is telling us that a new man is approaching, the Hu-hanska-ska, the White Spider Man, the Daddy-Longlegs-Man, The Long-White-Bone Man. He is coming across the great waters, coming to steal all four directions of the world."

"How will we know him?" asked the chief.

"This new man is not wise, but he is very clever. He has knowledge in his legs, and greed. Wherever these legs step, they will make a track of lies, and wherever he looks, his looks will be all lies. You must try to know and understand this new kind of man, and pass the understanding on from generation to generation. My message is carried in the wind."

Iktome made his body into a small ball with eight legs, and from within the sky again appeared the fine strand of spider web, glistening with dewdrops, and on it Iktome climbed up into the clouds and disappeared.

Iktome next went to the village of the Blue Cloud people, also known as the Arapaho. Again the chiefs and the people assembled to ask what news he was bringing, and he spoke in their own language: "I have brought you a message bundle to open up, and my news is in it. The Iktome-Hu-Hanska-Ska, the White Longlegs, is coming. I flew through the air to bring you the message, but this new kind of man comes walking."

The Arapaho chief asked: "How is it that you fly, and he walks?"

"Wokahta," said Iktome, "he is travelling slowly, going slowly from the east toward the south and the west, eating up the nations on his way, devouring the whole earth."

"When is he going to be here?" the chief asked.

"You will know by the star. When you see a double star, one star reflecting the other, then the Hu-Hanska-Ska will be near."

Iktome left the village and passed two women who were looking for wild turnips and using deer horns to dig them out of the prairie. They saw Iktome walking, pointing his arm skyward. All of a sudden, he drew himself up into a ball, and at the same time the thread of web from the sky hit the earth, and Iktome climbed up and vanished in the air.

Now, near the village of the Crow people, two old men were gathering herbs for medicine. They saw someone standing behind a tree and then saw him circling the camp. They said to each other, "He is not from our tribe. Let's ask him what he wants."

Iktome spoke in the Crow tongue: "The White Long-legs is coming. Look around you at the things you see—the grass, the trees, the animals. The Iktome-Hu-Hanska-Ska will take them all. He will steal the air. He will give you a new, different life. He will give you many new things, but hold onto your old ways. Mind what the Grandfather Spirit has taught you."

*The two old men said: "We'd better bring you to our chief."
They did so, and the Crow chief asked, "What message have you
for us?"*

*"The White Long-legs is coming! He will eat up the grass, and
the trees, and the buffalo. He will bring you a new faith."*

*The Crow chief asked: "Why is he coming? We don't want him
here; we don't want his new things. We have everything here to
make us happy."*

*"He will come, whether you want him to or not. He is coming
from the east," Iktome said.*

*One Crow woman gave Iktome a handful of wasna—jerk meat
mixed with kidney fat and berries—to take with him on his travels.
Iktome thanked her, saying: "You must watch this new man.
Whatever he does and says and asks, say "Hiya"—no—to him, say
hiya to everything. Now I must take my message to the west to the
Wiyopeyata."*

*Iktome stood in the center of the tipi circle. All the Crow chiefs
were standing around him wearing their war bonnets. A great
rush of power swept through the tipi. Iktome shrank into a ball,
and the thread of the web floating in the sky hit the prairie, causing
a trembling and thundering deep inside the earth. Iktome climbed
up into the web and was gone.*

*A warrior of the Snake People, also known as Shoshone, was
gathering his horses together when he noticed a man roaming the
valley. The warrior asked the man who he was and why he had come.
The stranger said: "I am Iktome. I roll with the air. I come from
Wiyohiyanpata, the east, coming with news." The warrior said, "Stay
here. I will bring our chief." The Shoshone chief came, followed by his
people.*

*"A new kind of man is coming, a White Long-legs with many lies
and many new things. If you want them, that's up to you," Iktome
said.*

The chief put two sticks on the ground facing north and south. It was a symbol for saying "No." The chief told Iktome: "We don't want him. Our generation is good, our nation is good, our land is good. We have no use for this new kind of man."

Iktome told him: "He is coming so if you do not want him you must resist him. I am going to Waziyata, toward the north, to bring my message to the people there." Iktome climbed a hill, and the Shoshone people saw lightning strike the summit, and heard the sound of many buffalo in the earth beneath their feet.

Iktome reappeared in the north, walking toward the village of the Palani, or Pawnees, pointing his finger toward their camp, shouting: "A new nation is coming! A new kind of human is coming! He is coming to this world!"

"Is it a newborn child?" a woman asked.

"No," Iktome said, "This is no little child. It is a man without grandmothers or grandfathers, a man bringing new sickness and worries."

"We don't want him! What should we do?" the Pawnees asked.

"You yourselves must know what to do. I am going back to my people."

"Don't go yet."

Iktome went towards the north with a large pine branch in his hand, pointing in the four directions, up to Grandfather Sky, down to Grandmother Earth. "Remember, this will be the plant of worship in the center of the earth, and with it you will see and know."

Iktome went back to his own Sioux people. He flew through the air, and the wind carried him into their camp. He told the people. "I am going back into the sea, the new man is coming, he is almost here."

"How will he come?" asked the Sioux chief.

"He is coming in a boat. You are the Ikche-Wichasha—the plain, wild, untamed people—but this man will misname you and call you by all kinds of false names. He will try to tame you, try to remake you after himself. This man will lie. He cannot speak the truth."

"When is he going to come?"

"When the white flowers bloom. Watch the buffalo: when this new man comes, the buffalo will go into a hole in the mountain. Guard the buffalo, because the White Long-legs will take them all. He will bring four things: wicocuye—sickness; wawoya—hate; wawiwagele— prejudice; waunshilap-sni—mercilessness. He will try to give you his new Great Spirit instead of your own, forcing you to exchange your own Wakan Tanka for this new one, so that you will lose the world. But always remember Tunka, the rock. He has no mouth, no eyes, no ears, but he has the power. Hold onto it. And always remember Tunkashila, the Grandfather, the Great Spirit! This new man is coming, coming to live among you. He will lie, and his lie never ends. He is going to make a dark, black hoop around the world."

"Is there no hope?" the people asked.

"Maybe, and maybe not. I don't know. First, it will happen as I told you, and with his long legs he will run over you. Maybe a time will come when you can break his dark hoop. Maybe you can change this man and make him better, giving him earth wisdom, making him listen to what the trees and grass tell him. You shall know him as washi-manu, steal-all, or better by the name of fat-taker, wasichu, because he will take the fat of the land. He will eat up everything, at least for a time."

Iktome left, and slowly people forgot that the White Long-legs was coming, because for a while things were as they had always been. So with time they stopped worrying.

Two Sioux women were out gathering chokecherries one morning after Iktome's visit had faded from their memory, a black smog suddenly settled in around them. Out of the blackness a strange creature emerged. He had on a strange black hat, and boots, and clothes. His skin was pale, his hair was yellow, and his eyes were blue. He had hair growing under his nose that fell down over his lips, his chin was covered with hair.

When he spoke, it did not sound like human speech. No one

could understand him. He was sitting on a large, strange animal as big as a moose. It was an animal no one knew.

This weird man carried in one hand a cross and in the other a fearful fire stick which spat lightning and made a noise like thunder. He took from his black coat something hard and shiny which served him as a water bag. He offered it to the women to drink, and when they tried it, the strange water burned their throats and made their heads swim. The man was covered with an evil sickness, and this sickness jumped on the women's skin with many unnumbered pustules and left them dying.

Then they realized that the wasichu had arrived, that finally he was among them, and that everything would be changed.[15]

"Why are you telling me all this? What am I supposed to do anyway? I am just one kid."

"You are but one person with much to learn, and there are others. Working together, much can be done. You must learn patience."

By this point I had had enough and just walked away. I walked along the lakeshore and over the bridge towards the boathouse. I had no real destination in mind, just walking. When I finally managed to get out of my own head long enough to be aware of where I was, I was standing in front of the Alice in Wonderland sculpture. I had climbed all over that sculpture when my school came here on a field trip from the reservation when I was just little.

I climbed up on the sculpture and ran my hand along the side of the mushroom where it had been worn smooth by thousands of hands. Alice sat tall next to me; she was the only one who really got me, the only one who knew what it felt like to fall through the looking glass.

I sat on the sculpture staring out across the park, trying to remember what it was like before I went completely mad: before I started seeing whole villages of people that could not exist, strange men in stone canoes, birds falling from the sky, trees dying before my eyes, rivers bursting into flames—before Ela.

They had been telling my dad I was crazy for a long time, but they had no idea just how insane I had become. I should give into my fate. I was crazy, that's all there was to it. I jumped down from Alice's perch and walked home. I actually felt a little relieved after finally accepting my fate as a rip-roaring madman. You're nuts, that's all there is to it, Trae. When I passed Eddy I gave him a quiet "hey" as I thought to myself *madman walking*. When I got to the apartment I did not bother to see if dad was home, I just went into my room, took off my clothes, and went to bed. "Madman sleeping," I whispered to myself with a little smile.

Between Alice in Wonderland and the stories from Ela, I had strange mashed-up dreams. I dreamed I was floating down a river, not of my own tears but rather a massive river polluted with all the animals that had been swept away by man's senseless acts. The river ahead of me was in flames, torching the furry, dead carcasses in hot, orange flames.

CHAPTER TWENTY-FOUR

I WOKE UP LATE THE NEXT morning, but it was all good, we were out of school for a few days for spring break. My stomach was in knots from the nightmares and I did not feel much like jumping out of bed and facing the world, a world full of brainless zombies polluting their own home. *Did I mention I woke up feeling a little bitter?* I finally got tired of laying in bed feeling sorry for myself and decided to get up and try to distract my mind with a little Forlorn killing.

At first it felt good to wipe out mounds of aliens, but after a while it seemed kind of pointless since they just kept coming. Eventually I lost interest, sat the controller down, and walked over to the window, leaving my character to his inevitable fate.

I looked down on the city streets; all I could see were metal monsters bellowing thick smoke and the walking dead, shuffling their way through the knee-deep garbage they had helped create. It was right about then I started to realize how bonkers my brain was getting over a silly dream. I decided I needed to get outside; my brain was starting to melt—it kind of smelled like burnt wires. I was going to head to the park, but I was afraid I would slip off my rocker again. I could not stand any more whacky delusions, I needed out of my head.

I hopped the subway and went to the Bodies exhibit at the South Street Seaport. At first it was really cool to see the dissected bodies, especially the ones posed as athletes, their muscles and tendons flexed and ready to spring into action.

I started to get a little creeped out though when I found myself alone in the middle of some bodies depicting various diseases. I started to panic and tried to get out of the area, but seemed to keep making wrong turns. I could not find my way out or find anyone else. It was like a freaky hall of mirrors but with dead people. I finally burst into the gift shop almost at a full run, huffing and puffing. The guy behind the counter looked at me with amusement but did not say anything. I looked around the gift shop at all the books, plastic brains, hearts, and skeletons until I caught my breath.

I really didn't feel like heading home yet so I wandered over to Asija's work site and was going to see if I could get his attention during his break. When I got to the site I looked up, but instead of being excited with all the cool construction, I was revolted by this unnatural mountain of steel spitting sparks from the welders and its massive darkness that blocked out the sky. I turned and ducked back out of the gate before Asija could see me. I used to love coming here to see the majestic steel walkers building into the sky. Man, my brain was screwed up.

I wandered up into the Bowery district, a grungy part of the city full of lost writers, artists, and poets milling about in coffee shops and poetry clubs. They were always talking but never said much. I went into the Beat Coffee Shop to get some water. In the corner behind the mic was a long-haired man dressed in black droning on in a deep voice. I was worn out and decided to sit and watch him rattle on for a few minutes:

The Crow:
 Sitting on the couch waiting for the world to arrive
 I watch the twisted reflection of the crow in the window
 His cocked head listening for pensive breath
 Quivering eyes
 First one then the other
 Watch every gesture

116

His heavy crest bellows with anticipation for a fleeting
moment
Before he flickers off the ledge
Disappearing into the dark night
The vibrations of his wings hang in the air
More felt then heard.
In the moment
I seek flight beyond the horizon

The people sipping their coffee listened, their heads nodding along until he finished then they all started snapping their fingers. The whole thing was almost cartoonish.

I was sick of watching and of wandering, so I decided to just catch the subway home. I went down into the tunnels where the thick smell of grease and fumes made me want to vomit. The sound of the screeching trains was deafening. I felt like I was going into the belly of a beast. It was weird, I had been in these subways thousands of time and never noticed what a foul beast the subway was. I could not take anymore and ran out of the subway covering my ears. When I got street side, I took deep breaths but could not seem to get away from the foul smells. If it wasn't the subway it was the rotten pile of garbage in front of the bakeshop. I started walking quickly towards home, almost in full panic mode. I cut through Washington Square Park, which helped calm me down enough to catch the uptown 6th Avenue bus home.

I was so ready to be home by the time I finally got there. I went in and flopped down on the chair and didn't care if I ever got up again.

I started dozing off when I heard keys at the door, "Hey buddy, let's go get a bite to eat. What do you say?"

"Alright, I guess." I stammered, kind of surprised to see my dad home already; I was not sure what was up with him lately.

We went down to the Stand, this amazing hamburger place dad likes. They have super juicy hamburgers, the juice just runs down your chin and all over, it's awesome. The best part though is the roasted marshmallow shake. It tastes just like a marshmallow roasted over a fire. I always want to order two, but usually dad makes me split one with him.

"So Trae, I got a call from your aunt today. She wants to know if we would like to meet her and Asija at the museum tomorrow."

"Museum?" *Gee that sounds like a load of fun...not.*

"The National Museum of American Indian History is having an exhibit that your Aunt thinks we might enjoy."

Dad at a museum of American Indian History? Something does not add up here.

"Come on, it's a really great artist. I have heard a lot of good things about her. It should be fun."

Art, well that explains it, dad likes to pretend he actually gets it, "The heavy use of line blah, blah, blah."

"Alright, I guess," I said with as much excitement as I could muster. I was not really looking forward to seeing Asija after today, it just seemed too weird.

CHAPTER TWENTY-FIVE

THE NEXT MORNING DAD WOKE me up early and we went to Murray's for breakfast on the way to meet my aunt and cousin. We went up the tall stone stairs into the lobby of the museum. My aunt and Asija where sitting on a bench waiting for us. Asija tried to say hi to me but I brushed him off. I was still all messed up from my visit to the construction site the day before.

I wandered from image to image until I came across a disturbing painting of a man lying on a dirty street. I could not tell if he was sleeping or dead, but other men walked by seeming to not even notice him laying there. Asija came over and stood next to me and started blabbing on about man's indifference to others and their world. I could not get the image of a giant steel monster bellowing sparks out of my head. How could Asija talk to me about man's indifference to man or the destruction of the earth when he was part of the destroying of it?

I walked away to look at another painting while he was still talking. I just could not bring myself to stand there and listen.

It was really awkward, so I wandered out of that area and into the area with all the headdresses, fancy robes, and a really cool drum with stars painted on it. The hunters and the monster bear were painted near the edge of the drum. There was a miniature layout of a traditional Mohawk settlement with its long houses arranged in a loose circle. It reminded me of when I imagined myself visiting Ela's village. I must have seen a picture of this before.

I walked over to a dimly lit corner where they had a few displays. One of the displays was a scene from a myth of how a boy lost his spirit guide. The storyboard next it told the story of the Elk spirit of lost lake.

In the days of our grandfathers, a young warrior named Plain Feather lived near Mount Hood. His guardian spirit was a great elk. The great elk taught Plain Feather the best places to look for every kind of game and he became the most skillful hunter in his tribe.

His guardian spirit said to him many a time, "Never kill more than you can use. Kill only for your present need. Then there will be enough for all." Plain Feather obeyed him. He killed only for food, only what he needed. Other hunters in his tribe teased him for not shooting for fun, for not using all his arrows when he was out on a hunt. But Plain Feather obeyed the great elk.

Smart Crow, one of the old men of the tribe, plotted to make the young hunter disobey his guardian spirit. Smart Crow pretended that he was one of the wise men and that he had had a vision. In the vision, he said, the Great Spirit had told him that the coming winter would be long and cold. He warned that there would be much snow. "Kill as many animals as you can," Smart Crow told the hunters of the tribe. "We must store meat for the winter."

The hunters believed him and went deep into the forest and meadows, killing all the animals they could. Each man tried to be the best hunter in the tribe. At first Plain Feather would not go with them, but Smart Crow kept saying, "The Great Spirit told me that we are going to have a hard winter. The Great Spirit told me that we must get our meat now."

Smart Crow finally convinced Plain Feather that he was telling the truth. So at last he gave in and went hunting along the stream. First, he killed deer and bears. Soon he came upon five bands of elk and killed all but one elk, which he wounded.

Plain Feather did not know that this was his guardian elk, and when the wounded animal hurried away into the forest, Plain Feather followed. Deeper and deeper into the forest and into the mountains he followed the elk tracks.

At last he came to a beautiful little lake. There, lying in the water not far from the shore was the wounded elk. He heard a voice say clearly, "Draw him in." And something drew Plain Feather closer to the wounded elk. "Draw him in," the voice said again. Again, Plain Feather was drawn closer to the great elk. At last he lay beside it. "Why did you disobey me?" asked the elk. "All around you are the spirits of the animals you have killed. I will no longer be your guardian. You have disobeyed me and slain my friends."

Then the voice said, "Cast him out" and the spirits cast the hunter out of the water, onto the shore of the lake.

Weary in body and sick at heart, Plain Feather dragged himself to the village where his tribe lived. He entered his teepee and dropped to the ground. "I am sick," he said. "I have been in the dwelling place of the lost spirits. I have lost my guardian spirit, the great elk. He is in the lake of the lost spirits."

He then laid back and died. Ever after, the Indians called that lake the Lake of the Lost Spirits. Beneath its calm blue waters are the spirits of thousands of the dead. On its surface is the face of Mount Hood, which stands as a monument to the lost spirits.[16]

I had finished reading the story and started pushing buttons to make pictures of the animal spirits light up then disappear and light up then disappear when dad walked up behind me.

"You alright, Trae? I didn't see you wander off."

"Yeah, I'm fine. I just got bored, that's all."

"Alright," dad said. "Your cousin and aunt had to take off. They said to tell you goodbye."

"Alright."

"Well, let's head home then," dad said almost disappointedly.

Dad seemed sad that I was not more exited about the museum and decided that we needed to go eat at this strange old building where some general or other used to eat when he was in charge of a bunch of soldiers. I tried my best to act excited, I did not want to disappoint dad anymore. It was kind of cool. It had war pictures and memorabilia. The floors were really old and rickety. It looked like one of those houses from the scary black and white movies they show on cable late at night.

Dad tried to talk to me about what was going on in my life, but I was afraid to even start to try to explain the crazy things that have been going on in my twisted little brain so I talked about my video games, the drums at the museum, baseball—anything to stay away from reality.

Getting dad talking about baseball got the attention off me. By the time we got home I could barely keep my eyes open. Dad was still rattling on about the ERAs of this guy and that. When I finally went to bed, I was too tired to even get undressed, and just flopped down on top of the blankets and was out.

When I woke up dad was gone but he had left a bag with bagels and orange juice for me. After breakfast I had to get outside, I had been cooped up inside all day yesterday in one old stuffy place or another.

I went into the park with an arm full of stuff, determined to not be inside until I absolutely had too. I had not wandered far before Ela appeared from behind a tree.

"There you are," Ela said, "I was worried when you left the other day. You seemed terribly upset."

"Do you think?" I said, really annoyed. Ela just blinked at me, unsure what to say. "You tell me the world is ending in a fire ball of dead birds and hey, by the way I get to fix it. How am I supposed to feel? And on top of that, you won't even tell me what it is I am supposed to do!"

I kept walking past Ela until I hit the trail. Someone had leaned a really nice wooden bat against a tree. I did not see anyone around, so I picked it up and started swinging it as I walked.

Ela followed after me, "You must be patient Trae."

"You keep telling me that, but why?" I said as I swung the bat and hit a tree.

"You have much to learn before you will be ready to take your place within the seventh generation. I have much to share with you."

"Maybe I should just take it." I said as I swung the bat and hit another tree, sending splinters flying.

"The bat?"

"That's right. I see it. I take it. That's how it goes," I said with as much nasty attitude as I could.

"Let me tell you another story."

I rolled my eyes and smacked another tree, sending waves of pain through my arm.

Sun had beautiful, wonder-working leggings that could set the prairie on fire and drive the game toward the hunter's bow. Veeho, the clever trickster, greatly admired the leggings, and one day when he came to visit, he sneaked off with them when Sun was not looking. Chuckling to himself as he ran, he said, "Now I can work many miracles and be the world's greatest hunter."

Toward evening he was tired from running. "Sun can't catch up with me now," he decided. He rolled up the magic leggings, placed them under his head for a pillow and went to sleep. He slept very well, but in the morning, he found himself back inside Sun's tipi. Veeho was too foolish to realize that the entire world is contained within Sun's lodge. Even though he was surprised to wake up there after having run so far and so fast, he was hard to embarrass

Sun smiled and said, "What are you doing with my leggings?"

Veeho may have been foolish, but he was never at a loss for an answer, "I just put my head on them to sleep softly. I knew you wouldn't mind."

"I don't mind," said Sun. "You can use them as a pillow if you want to." Sun knew very well that Veeho was lying, as usual, and

meant to steal the leggings again. But he only said, "Well, I must go walk my daily path."

"Don't worry about hurrying back, I'll keep an eye on your lodge," Veeho said.

As soon as he could no longer see Sun, Veeho ran off with the leggings again, this time twice as fast and twice as far. Again, he went to sleep and woke to find himself back inside Sun's tipi. Sun laughed and told Veeho, "If you're that fond of my leggings, you can keep them. Let's pretend that I'm holding a giveaway feast and that you got these as a present."

Veeho was overjoyed. "I never meant to steal these beautiful leggings, friend. You know me—I'm always up to some trick; I was only fooling. But now that you've given them to me of your own free will, I gladly accept."

Veeho could hardly wait to get away from Sun's lodge and put on the leggings. He put them on and ran over the prairie and ignited the grass to drive the buffalo toward him. But Veeho did not have Sun's power; he couldn't handle such a big fire. It scorched his soles and blistered his feet. "Friend Sun, come and help me!" he cried. "Help your poor friend! Where are you Sun? Come put the fire out!"

Sun pretended not to hear Veeho and soon the leggings were on fire. Veeho cried from the pain as he ran and plunged into the nearest stream. By then it was too late; the leggings were ruined and Veeho's legs were badly blistered.

When Veeho begged the Sun to make him a new pair of leggings, Sun said, "Even I can't make magic leggings but once. I am sorry my friend, be more careful in the future."

Sun could have easily made another pair, of course, but then Veeho wouldn't have learned a lesson.[17]

"Great! Another useless story!" I exclaimed

"Why did you come here, Trae?"

"To hang out."

"This is a huge city Trae. You can hang out anywhere, with anyone you want. Why here, why me?"

"What do you mean 'why you?' I didn't come looking for you."

"You would not see me if you truly were not looking for me. Maybe you need to think about what it is you are really looking for Trae." She said as she walked off into the bushes and disappeared.

I threw the bat off into the trees and walked back to the apartment. I stood in front of the building not really wanting to go back inside. I decided to walk around for a while before going in.

CHAPTER TWENTY-SIX

I WALKED TOWARD TIMES SQUARE. I could not get Ela's voice out of my head. I never went there looking for her; I didn't ask to be a part of all this seventh-generation bull.

I walked down through Times Square with its two billion people milling about in a sea of yellow cabs and flashing lights. I used to like Times Square but today it seemed so different. It was crowded and dirty. I wandered down 42nd Street. I passed a construction site with its big blue walls and small fenced windows, a few random movie and concert posters plastered to the wall. I studied the posters and decided to add my own post. I wrote "Decaying City" in large graffiti letters before slipping my pen back in my pocket and walking off. I had never done anything like that before—well, other than drawing on my desk at school a few times with a pencil, of course. I was kind of shocked I had just done that and a little excited by the rush of getting away with it. I was fairly sure I had not solved anything, but I sure felt a little better.

It burned off enough anger at Ela that I was more hungry than outraged by the time I circled back home. Dad had just gotten there, and we ordered out for hamburgers again. Dad tried to talk to me during dinner, but I just didn't want to be bothered, so I finished eating as fast as I could and went straight to my room.

Needless to say, I had more strange dreams. There is nothing like dreams about being chased by the New York Police Department's S.W.A.T. dogs while spray painting a continuous red line across an endless line of store fronts to help ensure a good night's sleep. I went back and forth between that and a decaying New York City with crumbling buildings and no one left but me.

I had another very strange dream of a medicine man being tied up with a rawhide strap and covered with a buffalo hide. Weird, eerie lights flickered across him. I could hear a strange rattle and voices but could not see where they were coming from. *I told you it was really strange.*

The next morning, of course, had to be a school day. I slapped the snooze button on my alarm until it finally fell on the floor and I could not reach it again before I finally dragged myself out of bed and went to school. It was really hard to focus in class; I really didn't see the point anymore. I managed to make it through to the first bathroom break and was sitting in the stall when I realized I had my marker in my pocket. For some reason I decided it would be a good idea to write "death and decay" on the wall. The smell of the marker burned my nostrils. I was sure someone was going to walk in and catch me, but I finished my masterpiece and managed a clean getaway.

Mr. Taylor, the school janitor, must have found it because after lunch I could hear him outside our room talking to the principal and he was really pissed. The principal went from room to room asking the teachers about who took bathroom breaks, trying to find out what hoodlum had the most likely opportunity to act out their delinquent ways. Luckily for me, Marcus had been the last person in the bathroom before lunch, so they pulled him out of class and tried to pin it on him. I probably should have said something. There was a part of me that wanted to admit it just because I was pissed off and wanted the world to know it, but part of me was happy to sit back and let Marcus take the fall for this one, so I did not say anything. I kept my head down the rest of the day, happy I had managed to dodge that bullet.

After school I meandered around instead of heading straight home, searching for more walls I could take out my anger on since nothing else seemed to work. I started getting increasingly more into it, and my drawings started getting bigger and bigger with buildings on fire and zombie people. I had gotten so into it I kind of forgot to be careful to make sure no one was watching. I was right in the middle of zombie number four with one leg and no eyes when I felt a thump on the back of my head. I turned around and this wrinkly old lady was smacking me with her umbrella. She was not saying anything, she just kept smacking me over and over again with a wrinkled scowl on her face. I was more shocked than hurt, but got the heck out of there anyway.

I ran down the street, hopped the fence, and slid down the hill in the park. I was pretty sure she was not following me, but I was not about to stop and check. I finally got far enough away from pretty much everyone I figured it was safe to stop. I bent over to catch my breath; my legs where burning.

"Trae this is not the way," I heard someone say.

"What way?" I said as I looked up to find Ela standing in front of me.

"This is not helping."

"Who said I wanted to help?"

Ela just stared at me, her sad eyes searching my face. "Trae, please you need to listen. This is not the way. Be patient and you will find your path."

"How! By listening to your stupid stories?" I said as I looked back down at the ground. I had gone too far, even I knew it. "I'm sorry Ela. I know it's not your fault. This whole thing just sucks."

"I know Trae, but you must not give in to your anger. You can do this."

I sat down and stuck my head between my knees, breathing heavy. I felt like two big guys where standing on my chest. I breathed really deep a couple too many times though and started getting lightheaded.

Ela came over and sat quietly next to me until I got my head to stop spinning. "I don't understand what everyone wants from me, I am just a kid."

"You are just a kid, but you are a special kid. You are part of the seventh generation that will help put us back on the path of harmony with our world," Ela said as reassuringly as possible.

"But I have no idea what that even means, Ela." I said

"You keep wanting to jump to the end of the story before you even learn the beginning Trae. You must be patient."

"I am sick of all the strange dreams and visions. I just want them to be over."

"I can help you understand your dreams. Tell me about them."

I told her my bizarre dreams from the night before; she sat patiently listening until I got to the story about the medicine man, then her face lit up.

"You had a vision of the Cheyenne Arrow Boy ceremony."

"The what?"

After the Cheyenne had received their corn, and while they were still in the north, a young man and woman of the tribe were married. The woman became pregnant and carried her child in the womb for four years. The people watched with great interest to see what would happen. When the woman finally gave birth to a beautiful boy in the fourth year, they regarded him as supernatural. Before long the woman and her husband died, so the boy's grandmother took him in. He learned to walk and talk very quickly. He was given a buffalo calf robe and immediately turned it inside out so that the hair side was facing outward, the way medicine men wore it.

Among the Cheyenne there were certain medicine men of extraordinary wisdom and supernatural powers. Sometimes they would come together and put up a lodge. Sitting in a large circle, they chanted and went through rituals, after which each man rose and performed wonders before the crowd. One of these magic ceremonies was held when the boy was about ten. He made his grandmother ask if he could take part, and the medicine men let him enter the lodge.

"Where do you want to live?" the chief of the medicine men asked, meaning, "Where do you want to sit?"

Without ceremony the boy took his seat beside the chief. To the man who had ushered him in, the child gave directions to paint his body red and draw black rings around his face, wrists, and ankles. The performance began at one end of the circle. When the boy's turn came, he told the people what he was going to do. He used sweet grass to burn incense. Then he passed his buffalo sinew bowstring east, south, west, and north through the smoke. He asked two men to assist him and told them to tie his bowstring around his neck, cover his body with his robe, and pull at the ends of the string.

They pulled with all their might, but they could not move him. He told them to pull harder, and as they tugged at the string, his head was severed. It rolled out from under the robe, and the men put it back under the robe. The men became curious and lifted the robe. Instead of the boy, a very old man was sitting in his place. They covered the old man with the robe and pulled it away again, this time revealing a pile of human bones with a skull. They placed the robe over the bones a third time and lifted it. This time there was nothing at all. But when for a fourth time they spread the robe over the empty space and removed it, the wonderful boy sat in his place as if nothing had happened.

After the magic Ceremonies, the Cheyenne moved their camp to hunt buffalo. When a kill had been made, the wonderful boy would lead a crowd of boys who went hunting for calves that might return to the place where they last saw their mothers. The boys found five or six calves, surrounded them, and killed a two-year-old calf with their arrows. They began to skin it very carefully with bone knives, keeping the hide of the head intact and leaving the hooves on, because the wonderful boy wanted the skin for a robe. While they worked, a man driving a dog team approached them. It was Young Wolf, head chief of the tribe, who had come to the killing ground to gather what bones had been left.

He said, "My children have favored me at last! I'll take charge of this buffalo; you boys go on." The children all obeyed, except for the wonderful boy, who kept skinning as he explained that he wanted only the hide for a robe. The chief pushed the wonderful boy aside, but the boy returned and resumed skinning.

The chief jerked the boy away and threw him down. The boy got up and continued his work. Pretending that he was skinning one of the hind legs, he cut the leg off at the knee and left the hoof on. When the chief shouldered the boy out of the way and took over the work, the wonderful boy struck him on the back of the head with the buffalo leg. The chief fell dead. The other boys ran to the camp and told the story, which caused great excitement.

The warriors assembled and decided to kill the wonderful boy. They went out to look for him near the body of their chief, but the boy had returned to camp. He was sitting in his grandmother's lodge while she cooked food for him in an earthen pot. Suddenly the warriors raised the whole tipi. The wonderful boy quickly kicked the pot over, sending the contents into the fire. As the smoke billowed up, the boy rose with it. The old woman was left sitting alone. The warriors looked around and saw the boy about a quarter of a mile away, walking off toward the east. They ran after him but could not seem to draw closer. They chased him a great distance with no success before finally giving up.

People grew afraid of the wonderful boy. Still, they looked for him everyday and at last saw him on top of a nearby hill. The whole camp gathered to watch as he appeared on the summit five times, each time in a different robe. First, he came as a Red Shield warrior in a headdress made out of buffalo skin. He had horns, a spear, and a red shield with two buffalo tails tied to each arm. The second time he was a Coyote warrior, with his body painted black and yellow and with two eagle feathers sticking up on his head. The third time he appeared as a Dog Man warrior wearing a feathered headdress and carrying an eagle-bone whistle, a rattle *made of a buffalo hoof, and a bow and arrows. The fourth time he was a Hoof Rattle warrior. His body was painted, and he had a rattle to shake as he sang. He had a spear about eight feet long, with a crook at one end and the shaft at the other end bent in a semicircle. The fifth time his body was painted white, and on his forehead he wore a white owl skin.*

After his fifth appearance the wonderful boy disappeared entirely. No one knew where he went. People thought he was dead, and soon he was forgotten. The buffalo disappeared and famine came to the Cheyenne.

During this time the wonderful boy traveled alone into the highest ranges of the mountains. He drew near a peak and a door opened in the mountain slope. He passed through into the earth, and the opening closed after him. Inside the mountain he found a large circle of men. Each represented a tribe and was seated beneath that tribe's bundle. They welcomed the wonderful boy and pointed out the one empty place under a bundle wrapped in fox skin. "If you take this seat, the bundle will be yours to carry back to the Cheyenne," the headman said. "But first you will remain here four years, receiving instruction in order to become your tribe's prophet and counselor."

The wonderful boy accepted the bundle, and all the men gave thanks. When his turn came to perform the bundle ceremony, they took it down and showed him its sacred ceremonies, songs, and the four medicine arrows, each of which represented a certain power. Over the next four years under the mountain peak, they taught him prophecies, magic, and ceremonies for warfare and hunting. Meanwhile the Cheyenne were weak with hunger and threatened by starvation. All the animals had died, and the people ate herbs and mushrooms.

One day as the tribe was traveling in search of food, five children lagged behind to look for herbs and mushrooms. Suddenly the wonderful boy, now a young man bearing the name of Arrow Boy, appeared before them. "My poor children, throw away those mushrooms," he said. "It is I who brought famine among you, for I was angry with your people when they drove me from their camp. I have returned to provide for you; you shall not hunger in the future. Go and gather some dried buffalo bones, and I will feed you."

The children ran off and picked up buffalo bones, and brought them back to the Arrow Boy. He made a few passes over them with his hand and turned the bones into fresh meat. He fed the children with fat, marrow, liver, and other strengthening parts of the buffalo. When they had eaten all they wanted, he gave them fat and meat. "Take this to your people," he said. "Tell them that I, Arrow Boy, have returned." Though the boys ran to the camp, Arrow Boy used magic to reach it first.

Arrow Boy entered the lodge of his uncle and laid down to rest. The uncle and his wife were sitting just outside, but they did not see him pass by. The boys arrived in camp with their tale, which created great excitement. The uncle's wife went into the lodge to get a pipe, and it was then that she saw Arrow Boy lying covered with a buffalo robe. The robe, and his shirt, leggings, and moccasins, were all painted red. Guessing that he was the Arrow Boy, the men went into the lodge and asked the stranger to sit up.

They saw his bundle, and knowing that he had power, they asked him what they should do. Arrow Boy told the Cheyenne to camp in a circle and set up a large tipi in the center. When this had been done, he called all the medicine men to bring their rattles and pipes. Then he went into the tipi and sang the sacred songs that he had learned. It was night before he came to the song about the fourth arrow.

In the darkness the buffalo returned with a roar like thunder. The frightened Cheyenne went to Arrow Boy and asked him what to do. "Go and sleep," he said, "for the buffalo, your food, has returned to you." The roar of the buffalo continued through the night as he sang. The next morning the land was covered with buffalo. From that time forth, owing to the medicine arrows, the Cheyenne had plenty to eat and great powers.[18]

"You must find the patience to go to the mountain and learn your lessons before you can take your place Trae," she said as she walked away. "We will talk again soon."

I knew what she meant, but I was still frustrated and bothered by all the bizarre things happening to me. I was sick of the delusions knocking around in my head, the strange encounters and feeling like the world was crumbling around me.

CHAPTER TWENTY-SEVEN

I STILL DID NOT FEEL LIKE going home so I wandered down to the old carousel. I watched the horses whirling around, whipping the kids back and forth as they tried to land rings on the pole that would win them a free ride. It was nice hanging out there, the loud music drowned out the thoughts in my head and I could just not think for a little while.

There was one problem with this theory though—after a while it led to a throbbing headache. My head started throbbing so hard I could not think about anything else, which in a strange way kind of worked for me. I walked home and got myself a big drink of water and sat in dad's chair until my head stopped throbbing. When I woke up at midnight, dad had covered me with his overcoat and left a sandwich sitting on the counter. I was too tired to eat and just dragged myself to bed.

I had nasty dreams about black smog billowing out of tall skyscrapers filling the city with thick clouds that caused the trees to wither and the leaves to turn black. Dead birds covered in black soot laid everywhere. The few people left where all wandering aimlessly, coughing as they tried to cover their faces. I think I might have been better off not sleeping.

I was actually relieved when the alarm went off. I could hardly keep my head up, but got up and got ready for school. I dragged myself to school and was greeted by the principal at the door.

"Trae, you look really tired."

"Yeah, kinda." *Thanks for stating the obvious,* I thought.

"The nurse is here. Why don't you go lay down for a while? We will wake you up after we finish breakfast."

I went in and the nurse pulled out the old green cot and blanket. The cot always smelled like stale body odor. I had to roll around for a while until I could find that sweet spot between the metal poles that held it up. When I finally managed to fall asleep, I went right back into the nightmare world I had created. Flaming oil ran down gutters into blazing rivers. Windows were smashed everywhere and hardly anyone was left. The few people left looked more frightened and confused then I was.

"Wake up Trae. I think you are having a nightmare." I heard a voice say softly.

I woke up to find the nurse standing over me, her long brown hair hanging down just above my face. "You alright, Trae? You were breathing really hard, like you could not catch your breath."

"Yeah, I'm good," I sputtered out, still trying to get my brain to wake up.

"Why don't you go out front for a second and get some fresh air? That will help," she said as she led me outside and sat me on the bench.

"I will be just inside. Come in as soon as you start to wake up, alright?" she said as she disappeared back inside.

I stared at the apartments across the street with their bleached-out balconies and peeling paint. Reality did not seem all that much brighter than my nightmares from where I was sitting at the moment. I stood up to go back inside, but for some strange reason I don't really understand myself, I turned and started walking towards the riverfront.

I walked down along the golf driving range and past fancy yachts to the end of the pier where Mr. Johns and I had gone during bowling. I leaned out far over the water and watched as it swiftly passed by, losing myself in wave after wave sweeping across the base of the pier. I stood there watching the waves until someone bounced a ball off one of the poles behind me, startling me back into reality.

I wandered along the pier looking at all the yachts, thinking about how much these behemoths cost and how much they polluted the water. I went behind a building, pulled out my marker and started drawing burning boats with bombs raining down on them. By the time my marker ran out, I had covered almost the whole side of the wall as high as I could reach. I could not believe how much I had drawn. I walked down the side of the building and slipped back out onto the street, trying to not draw attention to myself as I walked away.

I thought about what Ela had told me about Arrow Boy and was kind of embarrassed I had just vandalized another building. My embarrassment quickly turned back to rage when I told myself I did not ask for this responsibility and I did not want it.

Heading back to school I passed Chelsea Market. They always had the big black SUV's lined up along the back for TV stars who filmed there. I looked around carefully to see if anyone was around before bending over and unscrewing the wire inside the stem of one of the tires. It was a little trick Marcus used to always brag he "does all the time," though I doubt he ever really did it. I stood up and kept walking as I listened to the hissing of air from the tire fade into the background. I turned the corner and found myself standing face to face with Mr. Johns, who was walking so fast he almost ran me over.

"Where do you think you're going Trae?" Mr. Johns said heavily as he tried to catch his breath.

"I was heading back to school."

"Where were you?"

"I just went for a walk to wake up, honest Mr. Johns. I was heading back to school right now."

"Come on Trae, you can't be out here wandering by yourself.

You are supposed to be in school!" Mr. Johns said as he grabbed my hand hard and started back towards the school. "I know you think you are the toughest guy on the street, but you can't just take off man."

I just stared up at him, happy that he had not come around the corner and caught me messing with the tire. By the time we got back the principal and all the crisis staff were buzzing around outside and inside. They all started talking at me at the same time, but I was not really listening, I was still running on a high from just missing getting caught screwing around with the SUV. I was raging against a world gone mad. I didn't really care what anyone had to say.

They dragged me down the hall, past classrooms where I could hear kids yelling to each other, "They got him!" They took me upstairs and sat me down hard in one of the chairs in the time out room.

Mr. Johns flopped down in his chair and turned to me, "What is going on Trae? It's like you lost your mind or something."

I just stared back at him, my body pumping with adrenaline.

"I wish you would talk to me; you have been doing so much better lately. Today it's like you just lost it," he said leaning in close to me. "What is going on in your head?"

I sat as far back in my chair as I could, trying to get away from Mr. Johns' heavy stare. "I'm just sick of it."

"Sick of what Trae?"

"Everything alright! Why can't everyone just leave me alone?"

Mr. Johns leaned back and got a dark look in his eyes. I knew I had gone too far. "I'm sorry Mr. Johns. I am just tired of people acting like everyone and everything is just here for their enjoyment. I am tired of people that treat each other and the world like garbage, alright?"

"Where is this coming from? I have never heard you talk like this before."

"Well maybe it's about time then!" I said as I stood up, kicked my chair up against the wall, and sat back down.

"I don't know what's going on Trae, but you need to let others in. You need to let me help you before you explode."

I looked down at the floor, my mind racing with thoughts of ways to lash out at this stupid, messed up world. I had no interest in trying to talk to anyone about what was going on. They were all part of the problem. Why would they help?

I think Mr. Johns got tired of wasting time with me because he got up, patted me on the shoulder, and went out into the hallway to talk with some kids passing by on their way to gym. I could overhear them trash talking about basketball and arguing over who had game.

I just sat there staring at the stained carpet and did not look up until the bell rang. When I looked into the hallway there was no one there. The staff must have all been getting ready to send kids home. I walked downstairs, grabbed my bag out of Mr. Johns office, and walked out of the building without ever seeing Mr. Johns or any of the other crisis staff.

I headed back towards Chelsea Market. I could not help it, I wanted to check out my handy work. I turned the corner where the SUV had been parked, but it was not there. I was disappointed until I looked into the garage and saw a couple of men in suits bent over, trying to replace the tire. I am not sure why I found so much pleasure in this, but it felt good. Let them clean up their own messes.

I was still wound up from earlier in the day and wanted to find more ways to get it out of my guts. I walked over to Central Park and went to the blockhouse. I pulled out the small assortment of markers I had gathered on my way out of school. I had just started what was to be my latest and greatest work when I heard Ela's voice from behind me.

"What do you think you are doing Trae?"

"Leave me alone."

"This is not the way."

"What does that even mean? You go on and on about needing to be patient and to learn," I said as I turned around angrily. "But you never tell me how!"

"You have truly learned nothing have you Trae?"

"Not from you, that's for sure!"

"So, you are going to go around vandalizing buildings and people's cars? For what purpose exactly?"

"Maybe just because."

"You are a foolish trickster, no different from the coyote."

"Now I am like a coyote," I grumbled.

Ela stared at me with disdain.

When our tribe, animals, and birds lived together near white people, Coyote was always in trouble. He would visit among the camps, staying in one for a while before moving on to the next. When it was Bear's turn, Coyote went at night to a white man's farm and stole the ears off the wheat. When the white man who owned the farm found out what Coyote was up to, he trailed Coyote long enough to locate Coyote's path into the field. Then he called all the white men to a council, and they made a figure of sap just like a man and placed it in Coyote's path.

The next night, when Coyote went back to steal wheat again, he saw the sap man standing there. Thinking it was a real person, he said, "Gray eyes get to one side and let me by. I just want to take a little wheat. Move over, I tell you." The sap man stayed where he was.

"If you don't move," Coyote said, "you'll get my fist in your face. Beware, wherever I go on this earth, if I hit a man with my fist, it kills him." The sap man did not stir. "Alright then, I'm going to hit you." Coyote struck the sap man and his fist stuck in the sap up to his elbow.

"What's the matter with you?" Coyote cried. "Why have you caught my hand? Turn me loose or you'll get my other fist. If I hit a man with that one, it knocks all his wits out!" Then Coyote punched with his other fist, and that arm got stuck in the sap also.

Now he was standing on his two hind legs. "I'm going to kick you if you keep holding me, and it'll knock you over!" Coyote delivered a powerful kick, and his leg went into the sap and stuck. "This other leg is worse still, and you're going to get it!" he said. He kicked again and his other leg stuck in the sap.

"If I whip you with my tail, it will cut you in two. So turn me loose!" But the sap man just stood there. Coyote lashed the sap with his tail and got it stuck also.

Now only his head was free, and he was still talking with it. "Why do you hold me this way? I'll bite you in the neck and kill you, so you'd better turn me loose!" When the sap man did nothing, Coyote bit it and got his mouth stuck, and there he was.

In the morning the farmer put a chain around Coyote's neck, pulled him out of the sap man, and led him to the house. "This is the one who has been stealing from me," he said to his family. The white people held a meeting to discuss what they should do with Coyote. They decided to put him into a pot of boiling water and scald him, so they set the water on to heat and tied Coyote up at the side of the house.

Pretty soon Coyote saw Gray Fox coming along, loafing around the farmer's yard, looking for something to steal from the white man. Coyote called him over. "My cousin," he said, "there are a lot of things cooking for me in that pot." But of course, the pot was only heating water to scald him in.

"There are potatoes, coffee, bread, and all kinds of food for me. It'll soon be done, and the white people are going to bring them to me. You and I can eat them together, but you must help me first. Can you put this chain around your neck while I go and urinate behind that bush?" Fox agreed and, taking the chain off Coyote, put it on his own neck. As soon as Coyote was out of sight behind the bush, he ran off.

After a while the water was good and hot, and the white men came out to Gray Fox. "He seems so little! What happened? He must have shrunk, I guess," they said.

They lifted him into the pot and the water boiled his hair right off, leaving Gray Fox bright red and hairless. They took off the chain and threw him under a tree, where he lay motionless until evening. When it got dark and cold, he woke up and started off.

After a while Gray Fox came to Bear's camp and asked, "Where is Coyote?" Bear replied that he did not know but that Coyote went for his water at some springs above Bear's camp every night at midnight. So Gray Fox ran off to the springs and hid himself.

At midnight Coyote came as usual to the springs, but when he put his head to the water to drink, Gray Fox jumped him. "Now I'm going to kill you and eat you," Grey Fox said. The moon was shining into the water, and Coyote, pointing at its reflection, replied, "Don't talk like that, when we can both eat this delicious 'ash bread' down there. All we have to do is drink all the water, and we can take the bread out and have a feast."

They both started to lap up the water, but of course Coyote was merely pretending to drink. Gray Fox drank lots, and when he was full, he got cold. Then Coyote said, "My cousin, some white people left a camp over here, and I'm going to look for some old rags or quilts to wrap you up in. Wait for me." So Coyote started off, and as soon as he was out of sight, he ran away.[19]

"So what?" I said.

"So you are not going to help change the world. You are nothing more than another trickster boy." Ela said with contempt before walking into the bushes and disappearing.

CHAPTER TWENTY-EIGHT

I GATHERED UP MY PENS AND decided to leave before the freak girl came back to give me yet another lecture or even worse another stupid story. My head was pounding with rage as I walked to the subway, hopped the pay gate, and got on the downtown train. *Where does she get off telling me what to do anyway?! I am so sick of her stupid stories,* I thought. I sat back hard on the plastic seat. The pain of smacking against it burned across my back, but it felt strangely gratifying.

I rode the train to the end of the line at Coney Island. I walked down to the boardwalk and sat on one of the benches watching the mindless masses passing by without a care in the world. *Fools.* I got tired of watching people wandering the boardwalk pretty quickly. I walked through the old carnival rides with their faded and chipping paint. The chains that drove the rides were so rusted it was hard to imagine them moving anything; they looked like they would snap if you even looked at them too hard. I walked back to the train and rode back into the city.

It had been dark for a few hours when I hopped off the train in Chelsea and wandered around until I ended up standing in front of the building Asija was working on. The site was completely dark except for one faint streetlight by the office trailer. I stood there staring up at the building, the top fading into the darkness, and thought about all the horrible things that went into a building. All the energy it will soak up; all the heat, garbage, and waste it will put out. The thought of this behemoth monster of a building bellowing out so much waste, made my stomach churn.

I looked up and down the street to see if anyone was paying attention to me before pushing the gate part way open and ducking in under the chain that was pretending to hold it shut. My heart was pounding. I was not sure what I thought I was going to do now that I was inside. I wrote, "End the madness against Mother Earth!" backwards on the window of one of the cranes so the crane worker would be able to read it. I split open some bags of cement and sprayed them down with a hose to make them harden. I pulled the stems out of the tires of one of the trucks and poured sand in one of the bulldozer's gas tanks.

I stood back and admired my work until I started hearing police sirens. I could not tell if they were headed my way, but I was not about to stick around to find out. I poked my head out of the fence and looked around to see if anyone was watching before squeezing out and running as fast as I could towards the subway. I kept looking back over one shoulder then the other as I ran, sure that the cops were hot on my trail. The sirens slowly faded away as I ran, but I was not going to stop until I was safely on the train.

I hopped the turnstile and ran down the platform just as the train pulled in. I jumped on and moved to the back corner of the car. I tried to catch my breath as I watched every door to see if I had been followed. As the doors closed and we pulled away I finally started to relax.

As the train swept into the tunnels I leaned back on the seat, tilted my head back, and tried to calm myself down. I could not believe what I had just done, and I could not believe I had gotten away. My mind was racing so fast I almost missed my stop. I slipped through the doors as they tried to crush me. I climbed up the stairs to get street side, my legs still shaking so hard I could barely stand up. The cool night air helped calm my nerves and by the time I got to the apartment building I was almost back to normal. I had to steady my hand as I put the key in the door. I managed to get it unlocked and was trying to pull the key out when I heard my father behind me.

"Where you been, son?"

I was still a little nervous and jumped back losing control of the key. "I was just at the comic book store."

"Are you alright Trae? You are trembling."

"I am fine! I just didn't see you there, that's all."

"Alright, well you know I don't like you staying out so late. You need to get right to bed."

I nodded and went straight into my bedroom; I was afraid if I didn't, he would see my crimes written on my face. I was edgy for a while, sure that every little sound was the police coming to take me away.

I finally managed to drift off to sleep. I had a strange dream about climbing on the crane and sinking into it, trapping my legs. When I tried to push free with my arms, they got caught all the way up to the elbows. I was stuck there until morning, when the construction workers found me. They tied a rope around my neck, pulled me out, and took me to Mr. Johns' office, where my father and the police were waiting for me.

CHAPTER TWENTY-NINE

WHEN I WOKE UP IT WAS just getting light outside. I was still lying on top of my blankets with my clothes on. My mind was racing, thanks to Ela and her stupid stories, so I decided to get up and take a shower before school.

I was dressed and sitting in the front room by the time my dad got up, which never happens. We walked down to the corner store where I got a toasted bagel with butter and a hot chocolate. My dad, of course, just got coffee. We did not have time to sit down and talk before dad headed off to work, which was a relief. I went back up to the apartment to eat. I sat looking out over the park, lit by the early morning light. It looked so peaceful that it made it hard to imagine all the crazy things that happened there. My mind drifted back to Ela and all the things she had told me. I thought about what I had done last night, and I could not shake the fear that the police were going to break down my door at any second.

When I left to go to school, I half expected to see them waiting for me in the lobby. I headed for the subway as quickly as possible, watching all around because, of course, the police never go in the subway, right? Everything seemed normal and no one seemed to be paying me any never mind. By the time I got to school I was starting to feel pretty comfortable that I had gotten away with it. I went to class and sat back, drifting off into my own world. I reveled in my own awesomeness. During lunch I went up to Mr. Johns' office to say hello. He was sitting behind his desk reading the *New York Daily News*.

"People are so stupid!" he exclaimed.

"What's up now?" Mr. Corfu asked.

"Just all the stupid things people do. I just don't get it," Mr. Johns continued. "Someone went down to a construction site in Chelsea and trashed the place."

"Why?"

"Says here the police found evidence that it was someone upset about the environment."

"Probably some wacko environmentalist," Mr. Corfu said as he walked out of the room, shaking his head.

"What can I help you with Trae?" Mr. Johns asked.

"Nothing. Just stopped by to say hi," I said, very nervous.

"So what do you think about it, Trae?"

"What?"

"Someone trashing that construction site," he said. "It is a stupid way to try to draw attention to your cause if you ask me."

"Well, what should they do?" I snapped back, harsher than I meant to.

"Doing what they did is just going to turn people against them. There is a right way and a wrong way to get your point across. Ruining things is the wrong way; educating, speaking out, doing something to make a positive difference—those are the right ways."

"Sounds like he spoke out pretty loud to me, if it made the papers."

"This person was nothing more then a trickster trying to outwit the police," he continued. "It sounds like they may have outwitted themselves this time."

I looked at him rather confused by his reference to tricksters. Does he know about Ela? What else does he know? How did I outwit myself, do they know who did it?

"As you know Trae, I am Romanian and, just like in your culture, we have many folk tales passed down to us from our ancestors. Let me tell you one:"

147

Fox thought he was a clever little fellow. He thought he was the smartest of all the animals and would often brag about how many wits he had. One day when Fox was feeling particularly full of wits, he came upon Owl on a branch.

"Mr. Owl," said Fox, "I am the smartest animal in the world. I am full up to the top with wits."

"How many wits would you say you have?" asked Owl.

"I have seven wits."

"Seven wits? That is a lot! I have but one."

Fox smiled smugly and went on his way.

A few days later Owl and Fox met again. This time Fox was running and seemed very scared.

"Friend Fox why are you running so swiftly?"

"The hounds have found my scent and now the hunters are after me."

"Where are your seven wits? Why aren't you using them to get away?"

"I used one wit crossing a river, but the hounds were not tricked and were able to pick up my scent on the other side. I am so scared my other wits have left me and I can think of no way to avoid the hounds and the hunters."

"Perhaps my one wit can help you. There is a hollow at the bottom of this tree. You hide in there and I will lie in the path in front of the tree and pretend to be dead. When the hounds and the hunters stop to examine me, you escape. This time stay in the river until the hunters are gone, then come back to the tree."

Things went according to plan. When Owl was sure that Fox was safely in the river, Owl flapped his wings and flew away from the hunters. With no Owl and no Fox, the hunters had no reason to stick around and soon went on their way.

When Owl and Fox met back at the tree, Fox asked Owl how with just one wit, he had been able to come up with such a wonderful plan when Fox's seven wits had failed.

"I may have only one wit, but it is a strong wit, used to plan and survive. Your seven wits are disconnected. You use them only for tricks and games, so they are not strong and do not work together when they are needed."[20]

I looked away from Mr. Johns, unsure what to say and afraid he was going to see the guilt written all over my face. He seemed so convinced I had done wrong and had made a mess instead of getting people to wake up. I really liked Mr. Johns and it really bugged me that he was so sure I was wrong.

I went back to class and put my head down on the desk, trying to get it all out of my mind. Ela drove me crazy with her stupid stories, but maybe she was right. Maybe I needed to listen to her stupid stories so I didn't just screw things up worse, maybe it was already too late. *It's in the news now, surely they are going to figure out it was me.* They were not just going to let it go. They were going to hunt me down like the witless fox and lock me up in a cage.

I got myself really worked up until I could not stand it anymore. Sitting there was driving me deeper into madness. I asked Ms. Schultz if I could use the restroom and was halfway out the door before she even answered. I turned and walked straight out the front door without looking back. I just kept walking as fast as I could, sure that Mr. Johns would be right on my heels. I could not face him again or I was going to break and tell him everything, I just knew it.

I walked towards SOHO and decided to hop on a bus to Battery Park. I went to the ferry terminal and watched the ferries come and go. I was so lost in my own thoughts that I lost track of time until someone passing by yelled out to the kids trailing them that they were going to miss the 4:30 ferry.

4:30? School was out. I was free.

CHAPTER THIRTY

GOING HOME AND FLOPPING down on my bed and not moving again sounded really good. I went into the subway, paid my way this time, and went home. When I got home, I went to get a drink and realized the phone message button was flashing. It had to be the school. I knew I was going to be in trouble for leaving, but you know what, I could not stay there any longer. Besides, maybe I deserved a little trouble after all the trouble I had caused. I ruined some guys tires, graffitied walls, trashed the construction site, and worst of all I had hurt Ela.

I debated for about three seconds before deciding to push the button and find out just how much trouble I was in. I expected to hear Mr. Johns' voice but instead it was Asija's voice that came out of the speaker.

"Hello Uncle Pete, this is Asija. We had some trouble down at the construction site last night, and I think Trae maybe involved. We need to talk."

My heart stopped. How did he know I had been there? This was way worse than I thought.

I raced around the house, throwing my stuff everywhere, *looking—for what? The markers? Traces of cement? I really didn't know.* I went over and banged my head against my bedroom door. "Think Trae, what are you going to do? Do something! Don't just stand here!" I shouted.

I felt like I was going to crawl out of my skin if I didn't do something, so I ran out of the apartment not even stopping to lock the door. I did not have any idea where I was going, I just knew I did not want to be home. I burst out of the elevator almost taking out the old lady from apartment 3C. Eddy tried to talk to me as I went through the lobby, but there was no way I was stopping; he was probably just trying to slow me down until the police arrived anyway. I walked as fast as I could without drawing attention to myself. All I really wanted was to put as much distance between me and reality as possible.

I cut across Central Park West and into the park. I went over to the blockhouse hoping Ela would be there. I needed someone to help me out of the mess I had made. I walked around and around the blockhouse, searching for Ela. I called out for her but there was no response. After a few laps I gave up and started walking towards the place where I had first seen her by the rock outcropping. I wove in and out of the trees and bushes all the way down calling out and searching for any sign of her. By the time I finally reached the place we had first met, I was in full panic mode. I was screaming out for her as I dove into the bushes where I first saw her eyes but there was nothing. I lay there with the other cast off garbage for a while, trying to gather my thoughts.

I was not ready to give up, so I back tracked to every spot Ela and I had ever been in the park. I knew she had to be there somewhere. I was going to find her and make her help me. When I finally made it back to the blockhouse, my panic had turned to all out rage. *How dare she ignore me? I am the seventh generation, here to save the world. She has no right to ignore me, what arrogance!* I thought to myself.

I decided to head back to the outcropping and force the issue. I climbed to the top of the outcropping, stood at the edge, and called out for Ela one more time. When she did not answer I yelled, "Fine! I can do this without you! I will just go on my own vision quest. I have seen the elders from my tribe do it." I sat down and tried to clear my mind and open myself up for the visions. Nothing came, so I stood up, paced back and forth across the ledge, and then sat back down and tried again. As the night dragged on, I knew I could not go home and that I had to stay here and seek answers. I had to figure this out.

I sat for so long that my back started aching, so I laid back on the rocks but that just made me cold. I sat up, trembling, and started to cry. I could not contain it any longer, the tears just started streaming down. I had screwed everything up! I tried to stop crying but that just made the tears come even harder.

I was sitting there feeling sorry for myself when I heard Ela's voice, "Why are you bothering us with your crying?"

"Ela please help me! Please show yourself."

"What do you want from us?"

"I want my vision quest. I want to learn how to make things right! I am ready, please?" I cried.

"You rejected our help. Why don't you go away?"

"But I need you!"

"You are disturbing us. You must go!"

"I am not leaving! I want my vision!" I shouted, but it was met with silence.

I fell back and banged my head against the stone and the tears started to really roll down. I started to sob out loud for the first time since my mother's funeral. "I don't know how to make this better!" I cried out, but there was no answer.

After lying around feeling sorry for myself until I started to even disgust me, I clenched my teeth and sat up determined to stick this thing out. I was going to get my vision. I didn't really have a choice. I had nowhere else I could go. I had left the apartment before I ate dinner, so now on top of being cold and afraid to go home, I was starving. My stomach felt like it was going to start eating my spleen if I did not get food soon, but I was not about to leave.

I was leaning back on my elbows, trying to find a comfortable position to wait this out, when a shadow passed over and blocked out the moon for just a moment. I was startled, but when I looked around I could not see anything that would have caused it. I turned back around just in time to see a giant black blur coming right at me. I flopped back hard, trying to duck out of its way. My head hit a rock and I could feel a talon pass just over my chin.

I sat up to look for what had just buzzed me. I could not believe my eyes. There was a giant black raven circling above me, getting ready to take another dive.

I looked around for somewhere to hide, but I was stuck on top of this stupid big rock outcropping. As it circled back around, I rolled into a small crevasse just deep enough that the talons dragged across my legs but could not grab me. I could feel a searing pain in my legs as I started to weep in fear. I reached back and rubbed my legs; they were covered in a sticky liquid. I pulled my hand up close, it was covered in my own blood. I was to afraid to look up, sure that I would lose my head to the bird's fierce talons. I could hear its wings as I cowered in my little hole. I rolled over to look up as he crossed the moon, once again blocking it out for a moment as his wings whipped up a mighty wind.

As quickly as it had appeared, it disappeared over the trees. I laid very still, trying not to cry out in pain, unsure if it was really gone. The cold stone seemed to be sucking out every last bit of warmth in my body. I pulled my arms into my shirtsleeves, but nothing seemed to help. I was just about ready to sit up when I once again saw the shadow pass over me as the bird let out a screech that sent terror through my bones. I sat up and yelled, "Alright, alright I am going! Please! Just leave me alone." I started limping down the rock. I stopped under the shelter of a tree at the bottom.

I looked around and could not see any sign of the bird. I leaned against the tree, my legs throbbing with pain. I thought about my situation, which had really not changed, other than gaping wounds to add to the list. I could not go home, I had to find a way to make this right and I had nowhere else to turn.

Bruised and bleeding, I limped back up the rock to where I had been sitting. I sat down and tried to look at the back of my legs. They were really gross looking, but seemed to have stopped bleeding, at least for now. As I checked out my legs, I think I started going into shock because the pain faded, and my stomach stopped churning with fear and hunger. Again, I heard Ela's voice, "Stop bothering us, go away! You are a very arrogant little boy, not worthy of our help."

"Please! I am ready, you have to help me!"

"We do not have to do anything for you, arrogant little boy. Go away!"

"No!" I shouted, "I am staying!"

My brain was pulsing with anger. The pain in my legs slowly returned and my stomach felt like it had shriveled up into nothing. The cold started to make my skin feel numb. I laid back and closed my eyes, hoping that maybe my vision would come in the form of a dream and that maybe dreams were beyond the reach of Ela.

I laid there thinking about all the things that had happened. The first time I ever spoke to Ela. Learning to use a bow with berry tips. The baseball game I went to with dad. All that now seemed like a million years ago. I thought about my mother and how much I missed her, how much I wanted to be able to crawl up into her lap and have her hold me, but that was all in the past now. I laid there and cried until the sunlight started to crest the buildings, but sleep never came.

"Why are you still here?" I heard Ela's voice rumble down through the trees with great rage. I could hear the mighty wings of the Crow flapping as its shadow passed over me. I rolled into the crack and screamed, "Alright! I am leaving!" The bird swept down and took a swipe at me again, just missing my back.

I stood up and started running down the hill. I could hear it closing in on me, but I just kept running. I did not stop until I was standing outside my apartment building, my chest heaving. It was then that I realized it had all been for nothing. I was going to have to go up and face my fate. There was nothing else left to do and I was too tired and too hungry to fight on. I swung the door open and my father was standing just inside.

CHAPTER THIRTY-ONE

A LOOK OF RELIEF PASSED over dad's face, "You are home! You're safe!" His expression turned into one of sadness, "What have you done?" he said in a low somber tone.

My father led me back to our apartment. As we stepped inside, I noticed my cousin was sitting in the corner watching us. I had no idea what to say, so I just stood there staring blankly at my dad.

"What is going on, Trae? I just don't understand what you could have possibly been thinking," Dad said. "Why would you attack your cousin's work that way?"

My mind was racing a million miles an hour trying to figure out what to say, where to start, whether I should even try to start. Dad just looked at me, waiting for some kind of answer. I dropped my head, "I don't know."

"You don't know? You just walked into your cousin's work and destroyed things because you don't know!" dad said, his voice starting to tremble as he tried to control his anger.

I stood quietly staring at the floor wishing I could just melt and disappear into the cracks. The silence had grown to the point I thought it was going to crush my brain, when my cousin finally spoke. "Where did these ideas about the environment come from Trae? I have never heard you talk about that stuff."

I just shrugged my shoulders, afraid to talk.

"When you came to see me at the site, you asked me a lot of questions about our history. Is that where this is coming from? Did

I somehow give you the idea that this is how to treat people?"

Part of me wanted to jump on that and blame it on my cousin, but I could not do that to him. I had already ruined his life.

I shrugged my shoulders again as I leaned against the wall and sank to the floor.

"Son, look at me," my father said in a concerned voice.

As soon as our eyes met, I started crying uncontrollably. My dad came over, leaned against the wall, and slid down next to me. He put his hand on my back, which just made me cry harder. My body was trembling, and I couldn't breathe. I thought I was going to vomit.

I could not hold it in any longer and started telling him everything. I told him about Ela, the strange dreams, and scary visions I was having. I told him about the birds falling from the sky, the trees wilting. I told him about the seventh-generation prophecy. I told him about my night in the park and the raven chasing me away from my vision quest.

Dad listened patiently. I could not tell if he believed me or not. I was sure he must have thought his son had gone completely mad, but if he did, he gave no sign; he just listened quietly. When I finished, my cousin sank down on the other side of me and they both put their hands on my back to console me.

My dad was the first one to break the long silence, "Maybe you and I should talk alone for a minute, Asija."

They got up, went into my father's room, and closed the door. I could occasionally hear their voices, but I could not make out what they were saying. I was so hungry. I would have gotten up and got something to eat, but I did not have energy left to stand up. I was so tired I could barely keep my eyes open. I felt strangely relieved after finally confessing everything to my father even if it meant he thought I had gone totally crazy. Maybe I was completely mad, but at least someone else knew.

My father finally reappeared from the bedroom. He came over, took my hand, and pulled me to my feet. "Let's get you something to eat. Your cousin is making some phone calls and will be out in a few minutes."

He fixed me a bowl of oatmeal. My stomach was in serious knots so it was difficult to eat, but I managed a few bites before I thought I might throw up.

My dad talked as I picked at my food. "The enlightened teachers have come throughout the ages. When we forget how to live in harmony, they remind us how we as a people were instructed to live."

It was strange hearing dad talk about our history after so long and I did not dare interrupt him, even if I really wanted to throw up from trying to eat.

Long ago, the Haudenosaunee Nations were at war with each other. A man called the Peacemaker wanted to spread peace and unity throughout Haudenosaunee territory. While on his journey, the Peacemaker came to the house of an Onondaga leader known as Hiawatha. Hiawatha believed in the message of peace and wanted the Haudenosaunee people to live in a united way. An evil Onondaga leader called Tadadaho, who hated the message of peace, had killed Hiawatha's wife and daughters during the violent times. Tadadaho was feared by all; he was perceived as being so evil that his hair was comprised of writhing snakes, symbolizing his twisted mind. The Peacemaker helped Hiawatha mourn his loss and ease his pain. Hiawatha then traveled with the Peacemaker to help unite the Haudenosaunee.

The Peacemaker used arrows to demonstrate the strength of unity. First, he took a single arrow and broke it in half. Then he took five arrows and tied them together. This group of five arrows could not be broken. The Peacemaker said, "A single arrow is weak and easily broken. A bundle of arrows tied together cannot be broken. This represents the strength of having a confederacy. It is strong and cannot be broken." The Mohawk, Oneida, Cayuga, and

Seneca accepted the message of peace. With the nations joined together, the Peacemaker and Hiawatha then sought out Tadadaho. As they approached Tadadaho, he resisted their invitation to join them. The Peacemaker promised Tadadaho that if he accepted the message of peace, Onondaga would be the capital of the Grand Council. Tadadaho finally succumbed to the message of peace. It is said that the messengers of peace combed the snakes from his hair. Joined together, these five nations became known as the Haudenosaunee Confederacy.

When peace had successfully been spread among the five nations, the people gathered together to celebrate. They uprooted a white pine tree and threw their weapons into the hole. They replanted the tree on top of the weapons and named it the Tree of Peace, which symbolizes the Great Law of Peace that the Haudenosaunee came to live by. The four main roots of the Tree of Peace represent the four directions and the paths of peace that lead to the heart of Haudenosaunee territory, where all who want to follow the Great Law of Peace are welcome.[21]

My cousin came out of the bedroom. "The Great Law declares the right of all people to be treated with basic respect Trae, even when they make us mad or when we think they don't deserve it. Alright, here is the deal," he continued. "I have made a few phone calls and all the damage can be repaired. I have talked them into not pressing charges, but in exchange you are going to have to help make things right."

I was so relieved by the idea of not going to prison I was ready to agree to just about anything.

"This is what is going to happen," he said as he glanced over at my father, "you will finish this school year at your current school. After school you will come straight to the construction site to help us with clean up and recycling work to help pay back for the damage you caused. You will also learn about the way we build our buildings and why it is important. First of all, we do only LEED certified buildings, which means we build only buildings that are friendly to the environment. They do not rely on outside sources for their energy or most of their water. They usually have roof top gardens to help keep the environment cooler. They are high density which means more people can live in a smaller space and have less of an impact on their environment so that we are able to preserve more of our old growth forest and open spaces."

He looked over at dad, who took over, "You will go home with your cousin after work and I will meet you there. You will do your homework and we will have dinner with your aunt and cousin before coming home. That will be your life until the end of the school year."

My cousin took over again, "If things go well at the construction site, I have arranged for you to volunteer during the summer with some friends of mine that work for an organization called the River Keepers. They work on protecting the Hudson River and its tributaries from pollution. You will go out with them and learn what it takes to keep our rivers clean and healthy."

Dad took over again; I was starting to feel like a ping bong ball going back and forth. "When you finish with them you will come straight home where you will do school packets that will get your education up to where it needs to be. Next fall you will not be returning to your current school. You will start attending the Environmental Sciences Academy in Brooklyn. There you will learn about the science of caring for our environment. After school, every day you will go straight to your aunt's house. You will assist your aunt in caring for her home and in exchange she will teach you the history and stories of our people. This will be your life from now on. You will no longer be treated as a little boy. From this day forward you are a man."

My cousin chimed in, "I don't know if you realize this Trae, but I am also part of the seventh generation. I too have seen the visions and felt the fear. You are not alone; there are many of us out there. It is time you took your place among us."

My head was spinning but I felt something I had not felt for a while—a sense of hope that things could be alright. Maybe I could make my dad and Asija proud of me. I might even be able to show Ela that her faith in me was not in vain. Maybe I could have a place in this world.

I GOT UP EARLY ONE Saturday before heading off to the construction site to work. I put the Jolly Ranchers I had gotten yesterday from Mr. Johns in my pocket. I hoped they would be enough to get Ela to come out and talk to me. When I got to the bush where I had first met Ela, she was already there waiting for me. I held out a handful of the Jolly Ranchers tentatively as I walked up. She just smiled and laughed which still embarrasses me.

"You finally understand and are taking your place," she said, taking several of the sour apple ones.

"Why didn't you tell me about my cousin? It would have been easier if I knew I could talk to him," I said, immediately regretting the tone.

"This was your journey; you needed to take it on your own. Answers given too easily do not teach the necessary lessons."

The young man from the village appeared at her side. "We are here for you as you progress. Now that you are on the correct path, you will see us in more places. Do not think your journey is done or that it will be easy. There is much work to do and as you learn you must teach."

They disappeared into the bushes before I turned towards home with a sense of relief and anticipation.

NOTES

1. Cherokee: The Horned Serpent
2. Passamaquoddy: How Glooscap Conquered the Great Bullfrog
3. Chippewa: Leelinau the Fairy Girl
4. Cherokee: Forever Boy
5. Cherokee: How the Ducks Got Their Fine Feathers
6. William Shakespeare: A Midsummer Nights Dream (Act ii., Scene i.)
7. Caddo: Coyote and the Origin of Death
8. Cheyenne: Veeho the Eye Juggler
9. Algonquian: Why Cricket was Burnt Black
10. Iroquois: The Hunting of the Great Bear
11. Inspired by Greek Mythology
12. Inspired by Romanian folk mythology
13. Kiowa: The Buffalo Go
14. Mohawk: Prophecy of the Seventh Generation
15. Told by Leonard Crow Dog and recorded by Richard Erdoes 1972
16. Wasco: The Elk Spirit of the Lost Lake
17. Blackfoot: The Theft from the Sun
18. Cheyenne: Arrow Boy
19. Apache: Coyote Fights a Lump of Pitch
20. Romanian: The Tale of the Seven-Witted Fox and the One-Witted Owl
21. Cherokee: The Peace Maker

Made in the USA
Las Vegas, NV
01 March 2022

44806794R00097